Traumatic Love

Also by Ellen Hoil

Safe Haven

Traumatic Love

Ellen Hoil

Traumatic Love

by Ellen Hoil

ISBN-(book) 9781948327701
ISBN-(epub) 9781948327718
ISBN (pdf) 9781948327725

Desert Palm Press
1961 Main Street, Suite 220
Watsonville, California 95076
www.desertpalmpress.com

Editor: Mary Hettel; Glenda Poulter
Cover Design: TreeHouse Studio

Printed in the United States of America
First Edition July 2020

Acknowledgement

I wish to acknowledge many of the people who have helped me with this project. In particular, are all my Beta Readers. The one who started this journey with me, Lee, stands out among them all, though the two that helped me over the finish line, Debs and Kim, were lifesavers.

My editors, Mary and Glenda, who have seen me through my first two manuscripts, continue to give me support, and are often the voices of reason in my writing life.

Mardhie, who stepped in halfway through to give much needed technical help.

In the law enforcement field, many people came forward to help me out of a few binds I created for myself.

There were also several people who offered their assistance as sensitivity readers, who I will not name for their sake, but who helped me better understand the life of a domestic abuse survivor.

To all of the above, I will be forever grateful.

Dedication

To my mother and aunts, who continue to be the strongest women I know, and the best role models a girl could ask for.

"Years of love have been forgotten In the hatred of a minute."

- E. A. Poe

Chapter One

NYDIA SLOUCHED IN A chair at the nurses' station with her feet on the desk and a keyboard in her lap. She had an office but preferred to be in the middle of things rather than tucked away, especially after a difficult trauma. It took half an hour to clean up from the mess of the last patient and her hair was still damp from the shower. She was reviewing the data of the patients she had worked on so far today.

Nydia was twirling a pen in her fingers preparing to write on the paper pad next to her when her feet were pushed off the desk. They landed with an unceremonious thump and caused her to sit up. She looked up to see Trudy, the head nurse, standing over her.

"How many times do I have to tell you not to put your damn feet on the furniture?" Trudy asked her, a glare on her face.

"If you didn't keep it so neat out here, I wouldn't have any place to put my feet, now would I?" Nydia rose to her full five foot, four inches and glared at Trudy.

"Don't bother with that look. It may work on everyone else, but you're just wasting it here." Trudy grinned at her. "It's not my fault you keep your office looking like a bomb went off. That's no excuse to abuse mine."

Nydia held the chair out for her. "Here, let it never be said I kept you from your work."

"Yeah, well the same for you." Trudy gave her a computer tablet as she sat down. "Here's a new patient for you."

"Why are you giving me this?"

"It's a chart. You know, one of those things we keep patient information on, most often pertaining to medical information." Trudy grinned as Nydia took it from her.

"Ha, ha, very funny. I mean, why is the patient here?"

"She is a thirty-two-year-old female, brought in by the police. She has a head injury due to a collision with a baseball bat. Why, I don't know. The report states she was unconscious for about a minute. All the vitals are in the computer, except for one."

"Which is?"

"She's gorgeous."

"I don't think your husband would appreciate that observation," Nydia said as she pointed a finger at Trudy. "Does this explain why my waiting room is teeming with police officers? I passed them on my way over here. Was there some sort of incident or trauma someone didn't tell me about?"

"No idea what's up with them, and as to the first statement, nope, that info was only for your benefit. As far as my husband goes, I plead the fifth. I only gave you that information since I wanted to keep you from drooling on her when you see her, because when I say gorgeous, it's an understatement."

Nydia tried to intimidate her coworker with an angry expression.

Trudy laughed.

Nydia stuck out her tongue as she turned and headed to the exam room. "You're a riot today. You do know I could get you fired, right?"

As she continued down the hallway, Nydia looked at the tablet screen for the patient's name and basic information. She entered the room with her head down and was greeted with a deep, rich voice that reminded her of the silky tones of a classic jazz or blues singer.

"So, will I live, Doc?"

Nydia shivered at the sound and looked up into bright blue eyes that contrasted with the woman's straight, dark chestnut hair and olive skin. Combined with the patient's statuesque frame, the woman's looks took Nydia's breath away and a warm sensation came over her. The hospital gown the patient wore didn't detract from her appearance. Nydia didn't realize she was staring until the woman spoke.

"Doc, you okay? Or does this mean I'm terminal and you're just afraid to tell me?" the patient asked with a grin.

Nydia coughed to hide her dazed gape. She tried to gather her emotions as she approached her. "No, you're not terminal, at least not that I can tell as yet. Let me have a look at you and we'll decide then, okay?" she asked as she winked. *I can't believe I did that. Trudy would have a field day if she found out, especially if it turns out this one is the suspect and not the victim.*

"Sure. Anything you say. I want to get out of here as fast as possible."

"When that will be is up to the police, I assume. In the meantime, let's look you over." Nydia looked down at the chart again, "Ms.

Powers."

"Call me Jo. Ms. Powers sounds way too stuffy. As for the cops, ignore them...I do." She grinned at Nydia.

Nydia blushed. *Did she just flirt back? I should be so lucky. I'm sure she has a boyfriend or husband somewhere. Get your mind out of the clouds and focus here. You're a professional, think like one.*

"Since according to your paperwork you suffered a head injury, I'm going to ask how it happened."

"My own stupidity?" Jo blushed. "Does it really matter?"

"I suppose we could leave it for now. So, I'm going to do a basic neurological exam. I'll start with some easy ones. What day is it?"

"Wednesday, and before you ask, yes I know who the President is, though I reserve my right to silence on that one."

Nydia let out a chuckle. "Okay, let me check your eyes since your verbal responses appear to be fine," Nydia said as she pulled out her penlight.

"Sure thing, Doc. Anything for you. I can recite the alphabet backwards if that would make you feel better."

"No, I think we can bypass that. Can you look straight ahead, please?

Jo smiled as she looked at the wall in front of her.

Nydia tried to ignore the woman's charm, but Jo was making it difficult. Nydia shined the light in one eye and then the other. She noticed Jo wince at the light before she placed it back in her chest pocket. "Your pupil reaction is normal, which is good. Are you feeling any pain from the light?"

"No, only caught me by surprise." Jo smiled but she didn't make eye contact with Nydia.

"Do you mind if I have a feel around the area where you got hit?"

"All I ask is for a gentle touch," Jo said as she looked into Nydia's eyes.

Nydia noticed again how blue Jo's eyes were. They reminded her of pictures of water in the Caribbean Sea. She blinked hard to bring her back to the moment and moved to Jo's side.

"Uh hum..." Nydia cleared her throat as she tried to regain some composure. She began to palpate around the bump on Jo's head. "Let me know if this hurts?"

"Ouch," Jo said when Nydia touched a spot right over her left ear.

"Sorry," Nydia said. "On a scale of one to ten, with one being no pain and ten being the worst ever, how would you rate that?"

"A one."

Nydia smiled. "Nice cover."

"I try."

Nydia moved her attention to Jo's neck, shoulders, and collarbone looking for any additional soreness. She was conscious of the smooth texture of skin under her fingers and the strong muscles as they moved under her touch.

"How is that?" Nydia asked.

"Good. You're very gentle. I like that."

Nydia turned her back to Jo for a moment as she blushed again. *At this rate, Jo will think I'm a high school girl rather than a professional trauma doctor.* Nydia moved next to Jo's side and reached around to position the stethoscope onto Jo's back. "Take a deep breath, please. Are you having any headaches?

"Nope, fit as can be."

"Sure." Nydia knew her voice oozed with sarcasm. As she leaned over, Nydia saw Jo's eyes were focused on her chest. "Is there something I can help you with?"

Jo blushed. "Uh, I was just wondering what the N. in N. Rogers stood for."

Somehow, I didn't think Jo was the type to blush so easily. She seems too self-assured for that. "Nydia."

"Well, nice to meet you, Nydia."

Nydia looked down at the name on the chart as if she hadn't already checked it. "You too, Jocasta." She let the words roll off her tongue in a seductive manner as goosebumps rose on her arms.

"My mother was a big fan of Greek tragedies," Jo said with a grin that didn't hide her blush.

"I love a good tragedy myself. *Electra* is my all-time favorite."

Jo snorted.

Nydia stared at her.

"Private joke, sorry. Like I said earlier, call me Jo. All my friends do."

"Right," Nydia said, trying to keep her tone neutral, though her mouth was dry. She gave herself a mental slap to pull herself back into her professional persona. She began to feel around the wound again when she felt a small electric shock and pulled her fingers back. "Sorry, must be some static electricity. Are you feeling any numbness or weakness on your left side, in your neck, shoulders or arm, anywhere?"

"No, not at all. I feel fine." Jo lifted her arm and made a fist.

Nydia couldn't help but admire the flex of muscle. *This is ridiculous, she's a patient after all. I admit she's attractive, but no, end of story.* Nydia mentally shook her head. "How long were you unconscious?"

"I don't know. The last thing I remember was talking to Duncan."

"Duncan?" Nydia asked.

"He's my partner in crime," Jo said with a chuckle.

"Do you remember getting hit?"

"No, I think it was from behind. I just remember everyone standing over me. I tried to refuse to go with the EMTs when they started to put me in one of those neck contraptions and on a backboard. Anyway, they insisted I come in, but I want the record to reflect I got here without all that crap."

"Well, you have a nice concussion. Based on your examination so far, I don't think there is any extensive damage. However, I would like to get some x-rays," Nydia said as she made notes on the tablet.

"Sorry, Doc, I don't do hospitals. I'll sign whatever you need, but I have to go."

"Jo, I don't think you realize the risk here. If you develop any complications, you need to be in the hospital so we can deal with them. I would feel better if you were here for me to monitor, at least for a short time." Nydia rested her hand on Jo's arm. It felt warm under her fingers.

"As appealing as that offer sounds, I really can't stay. Give it up, Doc. You won't win this argument. Trust me," Jo said with a glint in her eyes as she looked at Nydia's hand.

"Is there at least someone at home that can watch you?" Nydia let go of Jo's arm. She was surprised at herself for feeling disappointed that Jo wouldn't stay.

"Yes, I'll be under good care. I live with my mother and sister."

"Okay, I can't force you to stay. I'll give you some instructions for you to take with you, and you'll have to sign our 'Against Medical Advice' form. If you feel nauseous, dizzy, or have trouble with numbness or weakness, please come right back."

"Sure thing, Doc. No worries."

"Well, then I'll give you everything you need to get out of here. I assume the police will want to talk to you."

"Nah, they know where to find me. No problem there."

Nydia finished her notations as she left the room. She went to the nurses' station to put together the packet of papers for Jo. She was having a strange effect on Nydia and the sooner they parted the better.

***

After Nydia left, Jo hopped off the exam table to get herself together. She regretted her hurry to get moving as a slight wave of lightheadedness hit her. She paused a moment, straightened up, and squared her shoulders.

Once she was dressed, she left the room and headed for the nurses' station. Nydia had her back turned and she jumped when Jo peered over her shoulder.

"Are those papers for me? Am I a free woman, Nydia?"

Nydia shivered and Jo smiled. *Nice to see I can affect her like that.*

Nydia turned and Jo didn't miss the up and down look Nydia gave her. She also didn't miss the lingering look Nydia gave the gold police detective shield attached to her waist. Jo watched Nydia's face pale.

Nydia's voice took on an icy tone. "Dr. Rogers, thank you very much. I would also suggest that you take your cheering section with you when you leave."

Jo was shocked at the sudden change in Nydia's manner. "I'm sorry Dr. Rogers. Have I done something to upset you? I thought we were getting along quite well." *She seemed receptive to the playing before. I don't think I offended her. The Doc gave as good as she got.*

"No, everything is fine, Ms. Powers."

"Well, I was wondering if you would like to join me for a cup of coffee, or dinner sometime? I mean, if that's all right with you? You don't have to or anything," Jo asked, despite the icy demeanor Nydia gave off. Jo started off confident, but the feeling left fast when Nydia only stared at her.

"Thank you, but no." Nydia grabbed the papers off the desk and turned back to Jo. "Please sign this here, and here." Nydia placed a pile of papers on the desk. "These include the instructions you'll need. If you have any questions, I'm sure Nurse Swenson would be happy to help you."

Nydia grabbed a tablet off the desk and left.

Jo stood watching Nydia's retreating form. Jo's shoulders slumped and she bowed her head as she walked away. She ignored her fellow officers waiting in the ER waiting room as she made her way to the door.

***

Jo sat in the cruiser as Duncan drove to the station. "So, are you okay?"

She didn't answer but instead looked out the passenger window confused. She hated confusion. It always put her off balance. *It's so bizarre. I thought it was going great. When did it go off track?* She shook her head to clear off the encounter.

Duncan glanced over at her. "So, are you all right? What did the doctor say?"

She sighed and turned to her partner. "Nothing important. I need to take it easy for a day. Once we get to the station, I'll finish out my shift doing the paperwork for this. I'd rather be on the streets, but it's better than the alternative. The prospect of sitting at home doing nothing is not appealing."

"I don't know, Jo. I mean, I understand you live and breathe this stuff, but maybe you should take the rest of the day off. Let your family pamper you for an afternoon. You took a pretty hard hit to the head. Anyway, I'm not sure you'll get much of a choice. You know the procedure."

"Nah, I'm okay. Nothing a couple of aspirin won't fix. I'm sure I can talk the captain into it." Jo smiled at him, but Duncan didn't look convinced. "Thanks, by the way, for keeping the whole department from showing up."

"Yeah, I tried to get everyone to stay away, but the ones on scene insisted. At least the captain agreed to wait to see you once I told him you seemed okay. Still, I think you should take the rest of the shift off. What did that doctor say?"

Jo turned away as a sad smile came to her face. "Oh, she just said to take it easy for a while. I can do that sitting in the station. I have reports to finish up."

"Don't try to hide it, Jo. I know you too well. Did you get a date out of her?"

"Nah, not my type," she said, trying to downplay the emotions she was feeling. "Smart women don't appeal to me."

"I never knew a woman who didn't."

Jo looked at him. "Yeah, well now you know. Besides, this one was a bit of an ice princess. I don't go in for that, too much effort involved."

They rode the rest of the way to the station in silence.

***

After a half-hour Nydia figured Jo was gone long enough, that it was safe to return to the desk.

"What the hell was that all about?" Trudy asked as she put the last of Jo's information into the computer.

"You know I don't get along with cops. So, I'm damn well not dating one. Besides, it would be unethical to socialize with a patient. You know that as well as I do."

"So, what was that?"

"What are you talking about?" She nervously pushed her hair behind her ear.

"You know what I'm talking about, Nydia. You and Ms. Cop, what happened?" Trudy said, putting her hands on her hips.

"I told you before. I don't go out with patients, especially not police officers." Nydia flung the papers she had in her hand down onto the nurses' desk as she started to lose her patience.

"The fact that she was, and I repeat was, a patient isn't the issue. It's that you're letting your family dictate your life."

"My family has nothing to do with this." Nydia's hands balled into fists.

Trudy crossed her arms across her chest. "Oh. Right. They don't. I forgot. I can't believe you would let them do that to you. It's been over fifteen years since you've had a real conversation with any of them. Yet you still let them influence your life."

"No, they don't. I just choose not to associate with some people. Now if you'll excuse me, I have things to do." Nydia pushed past her friend and rushed toward the solitude of her office. Once there, she took a fresh lab coat from her closet. The one she had on suddenly felt dirty to her. She slammed the door in frustration as she hung her head and sighed and considered what had happened.

I'll need to apologize to Trudy. I wish I could get those people out of my head, but I don't think I can. It's been so long. I wouldn't know where to even start. But to have someone like Jo in my life would have been nice.

Chapter Two

JO WALKED INTO THE clamor of the Riverview Police Department squad room. She heard one handcuffed suspect dismissing the accounts of his alleged car theft. She laughed at his creativity as she walked toward her desk.

"Powers, in my office, right now," Captain Scruton said.

Jo entered the office with apprehension. The captain motioned for her to take a seat.

"So, I understand you took a pretty bad hit today, Detective Powers."

"Not really, sir. More of a glancing blow."

Captain Scruton looked at his computer screen for a moment. "That's odd. It says here, according to Detective Reilly, you took a hit to the head with a baseball bat and were knocked unconscious. That seems to me as if it was more than just a little love tap. You'll need to write a report on this. Is there anything I won't find in your report when it's complete? I don't want you covering for the rookie who let you get hurt. He's already had his ass chewed and will be up before the review board." He stared at her with his brows furrowed.

Jo's leg jiggled up and down. "No, sir."

"What did the doctor say? Before you think of saying you're fine, don't, or I'll send you down to the hospital again."

Jo cringed at the idea of having to face Dr. Rogers again. The sense of loss over the doctor's rebuff baffled her. "They said some rest was in order. Other than this headache, I feel fine. I figured I could sit at my desk and get caught up."

The captain frowned and Jo began shifting under his intent stare. He tilted his head and eyed her up and down for a moment.

"I don't think so. As much as I could use you around here, I'm sending you home as soon as you've checked in with Reilly. If you want, write a preliminary statement, and I mean very preliminary, but then get your ass home."

"But, sir, honest, I'm fine. I promise I won't do anything other than sit at my desk, and the most I'll do is pick up a stapler. Please don't make me go home. You know what will happen once they find out. Being here is much safer, I swear." She held three fingers up in a Boy Scout oath.

"Look, Powers, you know I think you're one of the best detectives I have. I do."

Jo took in a deep breath in anticipation that this might be good news.

"But I also can't afford to have you get worse because you didn't take care of yourself."

Jo sat back. She stared at the floor for a moment, resigned to the fact she would have to leave work. "Yes, Captain. Can I ask what happened after I left the scene? I wasn't even sure who hit me until Reilly told me it was the perp's wife."

"It was, according to the other personnel on scene." He sighed. Jo knew he didn't like the situation. "She and the husband were brought in and are being processed now. Your partner should have more details."

"Thank you, sir. I'll go over the report with him and do a statement."

"No, the preliminary statement will suffice for now. You can rehash the rest when you come back. Make it fast, Detective. I want you out that door and on your way home within the next hour, tops."

"Thank you, sir." Jo left the office and found comfort in the squad room. As she surveyed the room, she relaxed into the hustle and bustle. She took a deep breath and absorbed the noise and activity around her.

Duncan sat at his desk talking to Jeanie Butler, the victim they had gone to help. Instead of being home where she belonged, she was handcuffed to a desk. She wore bruises both old and new, her left eye was swollen almost shut, and her right arm was in a sling.

The woman turned and stared at Jo with her good eye. Jo was used to the glares of hatred, anger, and disdain, but they hurt a bit more coming from the people she was trying to serve and protect. She blew out a deep breath, opened her email, and began scrolling through. Jo had promised the captain she wouldn't work, but since she had to wait to talk to Duncan, she figured she might as well.

"Stupid ass cop. If you had just minded your own damn business, instead of barging in, I'd still be home watching TV," Jeanie Butler said.

Jo sighed. "Mrs. Butler, if I had 'minded my own damn business' you'd most likely be at the hospital being treated for more injuries than you have, or worse, lying dead on your living room floor. Based on what

I saw, I would guess dead."

Duncan leaned in. "You're in enough trouble as it is, Jeanie, don't add to it."

The partners looked at each other. They knew what was coming next.

"Dwayne was just drunk. I didn't have more beer in the house. I wasn't able to get to the store in time. I had to get dinner started. It was my fault. He was just blowing off steam because his work cut back his hours, claimed he was drunk on the job last week. That's all. It would have been fine. There was no need to arrest him."

"We had every right to arrest your husband, and you should know that." Jo knew the futility of asking but did anyway. "What I don't get is why you would defend a man who nearly beat you to death?"

"Because he loves me. I know him. He's my husband. It wasn't his fault. If I hadn't of gotten him angry, none of this would've happened. I wasn't about to let you arrest him for something he had no control over. He only does it when he's been drinking. Once he sobered up, things would've been okay. Besides, I can take care of myself. I've been married for five years now. I know how to handle him, and I didn't need any help from you people. We're a family. I'm not one of those women who gets abused all of the time."

Jo stared at Jeanie. It was almost always the same story when the victim refused to press charges or cooperate. *It boggles my mind.*

Duncan finished typing and signaled for one of the uniformed officers to come collect Jeanie.

"So, what happened? The last thing I remember was handcuffing the distinguished Mr. Butler," Jo asked once Mrs. Butler was out of earshot.

Duncan cringed and then closed his eyes for a moment. "It happened pretty quick. As you were handcuffing Mr. Butler, Officers Fisher and Rodriguez were dealing with Mrs. Butler, taking her statement, the usual. Fisher forgot the most basic rule and took his eyes off her when Rodriguez turned to let the EMTs by. Mrs. Butler pushed past Fisher and grabbed the bat from the floor. Before anyone knew what was happening, she took a swing at your head. Lucky for us all, she is a righty and her shoulder was messed up by her husband. She used her left arm to swing so didn't have too much power behind it. That saved you from something worse." Duncan took a deep breath. "I hate to think what could've happened."

"Me too. Thanks for the save." Jo said. "It's a little weird to hear something you were a part of described to you even though you were there."

"I'm sorry about the whole thing, Jo. I should have seen it coming, but I was so focused on the husband, I didn't think to look behind you."

"It's okay, Duncan. If anything, it was Fisher. He should've known better than to turn his back on the vic in a domestic call, no matter the circumstances. You can explain it to them a hundred times and some rookies never get it. Hopefully he has."

"All right, but so you know, the Captain had a talk with him and from the dazed look of him afterward, I doubt he'll make the same mistake twice, assuming he gets to stay on."

"I hate to be someone's learning experience, but I guess some good may come out of it."

"Yeah, me too," Duncan ran his fingers through his hair.

Duncan was avoiding making eye contact with her, and she knew he was beating himself up about what happened. They had been partners for over five years, and he was as close as a brother would be.

"So, what did the captain say to you?" he asked.

"Oh, I have to write up my statement and then I'm out of here until Monday. Three days off, plus the weekend, actually two and a half counting today. Don't ask me what the hell I'll be allowed to do." Jo laughed. "Well, I'd better get to it. He was pretty adamant about me being gone fast."

"He's right," Duncan said as he looked at his monitor.

Jo noticed he still avoided looking at her when he said it. She turned her attention to her computer and started writing her statement of what she remembered. Within twenty minutes, she was finished—the remainder she'd leave for Duncan and the others to fill in. With a final tap on the keyboard, the report was saved and on its way to the records department. She turned off the machine and looked over at Duncan, who was busy typing and studying his monitor. She sighed.

"I guess that's it." She looked around the room hoping to find something to keep her there but she couldn't find anything. "I suppose I'd better get going."

Duncan looked up. "Yeah, well, so, I guess I won't see you 'til Monday. Take care of yourself. If you need anything over the weekend, give me a call."

"I will." She stood up to leave knowing there was nothing she would need from him, not with her mother and sister around. "Take care, Duncan. I owe you big. Donuts on me next time."

"Yeah, right, see you."

Jo turned and walked away thinking, *I'll miss this, but it's only a few days.* Jo shivered. *Wow, this could have ended a lot worse if it wasn't for luck.*

***

Jo threw her keys on the small table by the door and hung her coat in the closet. "Anybody home?" she called out. She breathed a sigh of relief when all she heard was quiet. She put the papers from the hospital on the counter in the kitchen. She felt queasy at the thought of eating anything, so she took a can of ginger ale out of the fridge and went into the living room.

Jo grabbed the remote off the sofa, turned on CNN, and laid on the couch, her long legs hanging over the end. She opened the can and took a swig of the soda, followed by a deep belch. She smiled, knowing if anyone else had been home, she would get a lecture. The commotion of the day's events caught up to her, along with the headache she had been fighting. *God, I'm exhausted.* She set the soda on the coffee table and closed her eyes. She listened to the newscaster drone on and in no time at all, she was fast asleep, dreaming of a certain doctor.

"Jocasta Powers, wake up this second!"

Jo bolted upright. The room swirled for a moment and she grabbed the table with one hand to keep from falling. She looked up to see her sister standing in the doorway to the kitchen, clutching the papers from the hospital.

"Uh, oh," Jo said as she tried to regain her balance.

"Are you okay?" Ellie came over and sat next to her.

Jo closed her eyes against the dizziness. "Yeah, I just sat up too fast, and what the hell are you doing yelling like that? You could've given me a heart attack."

"I'll give you worse than that." Ellie tapped Jo with a light punch to the arm. "How long have you been asleep?"

"I don't know. I got home around two o'clock. I laid down to watch the news and fell asleep. Why? What time is it now?"

Ellie shook the papers. "Well, that doesn't matter at this point, since it says here you're supposed to be supervised. You would have known that if you had bothered reading the doctor's discharge instructions, which I know you didn't." Ellie pushed the hair off Jo's forehead. "So, what happened? You should have called one of us."

"I took a beaner to the head." Jo leaned into the soothing touch. Her mom did the exact same thing whenever one of them was sick or upset. Ellie had picked up the habit.

"Where?" Ellie moved to sit on the edge off the table so she was directly in front of Jo.

"Here." Jo pointed to the tender spot on her head.

Ellie looked at it closer without touching it and whistled. "That is some bump you've got there. I'm surprised they didn't keep you at the hospital longer. What did the x-ray show?"

"Uhm, they didn't. You know me and hospitals don't mix."

"True," Ellie said, nodding. "I know you cop types. You get a sucking chest wound and claim it's just a flesh wound. So, how did Duncan even manage to get you to the hospital this time?'

"I was unconscious. I didn't wake up until it was too late to argue. If I had been awake, they never would have made it as far as they did."

"Ah." Ellie moved to the edge of the couch. She cupped her sister's chin and moved her head, looking in her eyes.

"So, what do you think? Will I live, Nurse Powers?"

Ellie let go. "You will, at least until Mom gets home and kills you for getting hurt. You know how she worries about you on the job."

"Yeah, I know. I'll have to put up with a lot of TLC over the next few days, won't I?" Jo moaned, resigned to the thought of her mother taking care of her every need for the next several days. If she were lucky, she'd be allowed out of bed to go to the bathroom.

"Have you had anything to eat since you got hit?"

"Nah. I was going to but felt a little unsettled when I got home."

"How about I make you some soup and see if you can get it down?"

"Sounds good. Thanks, Electra."

"No worries, sis, and don't call me that, Jocasta."

Jo smiled at the old play between them. "Why did they ever pick our names?"

"Mom's twisted sense of humor. I'll never believe anything else," Ellie said with a deep laugh.

Jo beamed. Outside her job, her family was all she cared about.

Chapter Three

NYDIA WALKED INTO WORK with her third cup of tea in hand. She still felt exhausted and cranky after more than a week of restless sleep. She walked up to the main desk of the ER and greeted the receptionist with more enthusiasm than she felt.

"Hi, Pam. How are you? Any messages or disasters I should know about?"

"Hi, Dr. Rogers. I'm good. There's one message from Dr. Stephenson. I put it on top. The rest don't look so pressing. As for disasters, nothing that I know of."

"Okay. Thanks." Nydia took the pile and headed toward her office, but before she made it to her sanctuary, her name was bellowed down the hallway.

"Rogers."

She cringed. *Only one person here is stupid enough to address me in that manner.* She stood straight and turned around. "Good morning, Dr. Goddard," Nydia said, emphasizing the title he failed to use on her. "What can I do for you this morning?"

"I want you to talk to that nurse about her insubordinate attitude."

Nydia took a deep breath and let it out quietly. "Come into my office."

"No. I want this dealt with immediately."

"Dr. Goddard, I don't think the hallway, in public, is the place for this type of discussion. Let's go to my office."

"When I come to you with a problem and I expect you to deal with me, and it, now."

"Follow me," Nydia said, stepping into the curtained treatment area next to her. As Dr. Goddard strode in, she flung the curtain closed behind them. She took a deep breath to calm her fury and think before she spoke. *I don't have the patience for his petty bullshit complaints today. Unfortunately, I have to be professional, even if he isn't.*

She turned to face him. "Which nurse and what did she do?"

"That Swenson woman. She dared to question an order I wrote for a patient."

"Her title and name are Nurse Swenson. What was the order?"

"That doesn't matter. It was from a doctor and the nurses have no right to question a superior in that way."

"Dr. Goddard, what was the order for?" Nydia asked. She strained not to let out a scream of frustration.

"It was for five milligrams of Compazine for a twelve-year-old male presenting with fever, vomiting, and lower abdominal pain on the right lower quadrant, if you insist on knowing," he said, standing up straight in order to look down at her. It was his usual means of displaying his disdain toward the women staff members.

"Did you check his white counts and rule out appendicitis first?"

"There was no need for that. It was a simple case of gastroenteritis. I resent being questioned on my diagnostics."

"So, you prescribed the maximum dosage possible of a drug—one only used as a last resort for children—and you didn't even check for appendicitis? Well, I'll talk to Nurse Swenson about her tone of voice, but as far as I'm concerned, she had every right to question that order, especially, if you hadn't considered appendicitis. I assume the patient is still here?" Nydia took a step past him and threw the curtain open to leave.

"Of course not. I sent him home," Dr. Goddard said.

"What?" Nydia's face flushed with anger. The muscles in her jaw tightened. "You didn't keep him to see how he reacted? I suggest, Doctor, that you call his family and get him back in here. If he does have appendicitis and it ruptures, then you and this hospital are at a huge risk. You can then explain to Risk Management why we may end up paying a multi-million-dollar settlement."

"How dare you speak to me like that," he said as his body stiffened. "I've never—"

Nydia cut him off before he could go any further. "How dare I?" Her voice was a low growl. "I'll tell you how I dare. I dare because I'm the Chief of this department and your direct supervisor. I'm the one responsible for the running of this ER. So, you'd damn well better make that phone call."

Dr. Goddard was silent and, if the wide-eyed look and the vein standing out in his neck were anything to go by, he was shocked and furious. She ignored him as she stormed off in the direction of her office before he had a chance to recover.

Nydia resisted the urge to slam her office door. Instead, she carefully closed it and leaned against it. She took a large swig of the now cold tea and let out a deep sigh. She fell in her chair and tried to let her anger dissipate. Ready to face her workday again, after a few minutes, she looked at the messages Pam had given her. The one from Dr. Stephenson, the Medical Director, read 'Report to my office as soon as you arrive.'

Ugh, now what? She finished her tea in two quick gulps, made a face, and stuck out her tongue to try and get rid of the foul taste the cold tea and milk left. She squared her shoulders and tried to recover enough to face her boss and whatever crisis he had waiting for her. Maybe she would get lucky and it was something simple. That would be a nice change.

***

"Go right in, he's expecting you, Dr. Rogers," Sara, Dr. Stephenson's secretary, said. She smiled as Nydia entered the outer office.

"Thanks." Nydia opened the heavy wood door.

Dr. James Stephenson was a man she admired. Not many men of his generation would hire a woman to head up a trauma unit.

"Good morning, Dr. Stephenson."

"Good Morning, Nydia. I see you got my message."

"Yes, sir. What can I do for you?" Nydia took a seat in one of the chairs facing his desk.

"Well, you can start by calling me Jim, as I've asked you to a hundred times before."

"Okay, Jim. Sir," Nydia said as she grinned.

Jim chuckled. "I know you're probably pressed for time, so I'll get to the point. I was hoping you'd be willing to take on an extra duty for me. I need someone I trust to be responsible in handling this."

"Sure, Jim. Anything you need."

"Good."

"So, what is it?" Nydia leaned forward, her curiosity piqued.

"The police have asked me to assign one doctor from each shift to act as a liaison for their Intimate Partner Violence Unit."

Nydia cringed. "Intimate Partner Violence Unit? What is that? Don't they already have a Domestic Violence Unit?"

"They do. This new unit deals specifically with domestic violence between adults and older teens in a relationship. The police are breaking the Domestic Crimes Unit into two separate squads, one for child and family abuse cases and this new one. You'll be the liaison and point person between the ER and the new unit. You'll treat the patient first, of course, but then coordinate with the IPV regarding evidence and anything else they need. It's pretty straightforward. If it becomes too much, let me know, then we can consider extra staff."

"Sounds like an excellent idea, Jim. I'll get right on it."

"Okay, well I'll let you return to your day, although I've already heard Dr. Goddard started your morning off well. Any particular reason it's in the grapevine already?"

"Yes. I tried handling the situation quietly in my office, but he insisted on making a spectacle and discussing the matter in the hallway."

"All right. As I said, I trust your judgment, Nydia."

"Thank you, Jim. Next time I'll try a little harder to have discussions in private. I promise. I'll keep you informed about how the project is going as we get it up and running."

As soon as she was clear of his office, Nydia took several deep, calming breaths, and wiped her sweaty palms on her lab coat. She had no idea how she was going to function in this new position. The thought of working that close with the police was overwhelming. Her normal practice when possible, was to pass them off to the social workers, nurses, or assisting doctors, keeping her interactions to the bare minimum.

Back down in the ER, she found Trudy at the main station. Trudy looked up when Nydia joined her.

"You okay? You don't look so good," Trudy said.

"No, but I will be. I have no choice. Not enough sleep last night and now a new assignment from Dr. Stephenson. I just need to get a handle on everything including Dr. Goddard."

"Why, what's up? There has to be more to it than just another project. Well, except for Goddard. He's just being his usual asinine self."

"You're looking at the new police liaison for the Intimate Partners Violence Unit," Nydia said as she sat down and buried her face in her hands.

Trudy put her hand on Nydia's shoulder. "Oh geez, Nydia, what are you going to do? I know how much you hate dealing with them now. How are you going to manage being a point person?"

"Nothing I can do," she said as she sat up, closed her eyes, and took a deep breath.

"I'll deal with it as best I can. I'm a professional, for crying out loud. I can very well act like one. Right?"

"If you need any help, let me know. I'm here for you." Trudy squeezed her shoulder.

"I will and I do. I'll need a nurse to assist me when the police need an exam done. You're the one I trust the most."

"Thanks for the confidence and you know I'd love to help."

"Oh, by the way, Dr. Goddard did have a talk with me."

"And what did the esteemed Dr. Goddard have to say."

"He wasn't too happy with either of us when I got done with him."

"I'll try not to cause you any more trouble. But for now, how about we try to get the board cleared?"

"Okay, we'd better get to it," Nydia said with as much resolve as she was capable of at the moment, and strode toward the first examination area.

Chapter Four

NYDIA CAME OUT OF the trauma room with Trudy beside her. She handed the tablet to Trudy and said, "Can you put that up with the others?"

"Sure. Is she finished?"

Nydia shook her head. "Not yet. I'm having her taken down for x-rays to see if any of the ribs have hairline fractures. When she comes back, we can finish. She should be back in half an hour or so. I asked Radiology to rush her through. But right now, there's no acute danger. God, I hate seeing kids like that. I assume Child Protective Services have been called?"

"Yeah. The police are waiting for them so they can talk to her. The father is already in custody from what I understand."

"Thanks. I'll talk to CPS when they get here. Point them to me when they arrive. Hopefully soon, since we're off the clock in a bit."

"Okay, no problem. You know, Nydia, I've been meaning to tell you that I think you've been doing really well dealing with the liaison situation. I know this case doesn't fall under that, but it made me think of how well you've been dealing with the situation. I thought for sure I'd have to clean at least one officer's body off the floor by now," Trudy said with a small laugh.

"Gee, thanks for the vote of confidence." Nydia lightly punched Trudy's shoulder. "I didn't think I could pull it off at first. I seem to be getting there though. Since we haven't had that many major cases like those lately, I've been able to keep it brief. Plus, the police have been behaving themselves for the most part, so it hasn't been too hard."

"I understand." Trudy said as she watched Nydia take her lab coat off.

"Thanks. I'll be in the doctors' lounge getting some coffee. Let me know when everyone is ready to brief the next shift and hand off the current cases. It's been a long ass day."

It had been a little over three weeks since she had become the liaison, and each encounter with the police grated on her. *However,* she thought, *lately I think I wouldn't mind running into Detective Powers again. There was something about her. Ugh, what am I thinking? Put any ideas of her out of your mind for good already. Move on.*

Trudy chuckled. "I'm sure having three traumas in one day will do that to you. That's what you get for thinking we would have an easy Thursday and cruise into the weekend unscathed."

"We only have twenty minutes to go. Then we're one step closer to the weekend. That's the nice thing about the end of the day on Thursdays, tomorrow is TGIF."

"I hope you didn't just jinx us."

"All the same—" Nydia was interrupted by the squawk of the EMT radio behind her. She put her lab coat back on and listened.

"Riverview Ambulance Unit 3 with a possible assault victim, female, multiple traumas, ETA four minutes to your location."

Trudy grabbed the microphone and began getting the victim's vitals from the ambulance crew.

Nydia stopped a nurse walking by.

"Janet, get Trauma 1 ready for an incoming, please."

"Sure thing, Dr. Rogers, I'm right on it," Janet said as she rushed off.

Before Nydia had a chance to do anything more, she heard the radio go off again.

"Riverview Ambulance Unit 2 to Riverview Hospital, we are ETA six minutes to you. We have a male patient with a compound fracture to his arm."

"Oh, great. Exactly what I needed right now," she said turning to Trudy. "Meet me in Trauma 1. Dr. Goddard can handle the fracture. Trudy, can you notify him, please? If he gives you a hard time, tell him it's a direct order from me."

"Got it covered."

An hour later, Nydia took her gloves off, threw them into the biohazard bin next to the door, and walked outside with Trudy.

"Dr. Rogers, the patient's sister is waiting in the family room for you," Cynthia, one of the LPN's said when she got to the nurses' station.

Nydia and Trudy went and stood outside the door. "Sometimes I think giving out the news is the hardest part of the job," Nydia said.

"You'll be fine, you're better at this part than you think. Take a deep breath." Trudy opened the door for Nydia.

Nydia entered the room and found a middle-aged woman sitting on the edge of the couch. She looked up as Nydia came in. Her eyes were red and puffy from crying, and she held a tissue in her hand.

Nydia sat down in the chair across from her and leaned forward, her arms resting on her thighs. "I'm Dr. Rogers. I treated your sister, Linda. I want to go over with you what her current state is, and what we are doing to help her."

"I'm Doreen, Doreen Samuleson. How is she? I can't tell you how many times I told her to leave that bastard. This isn't the only time we've been here. But it's never been this bad."

"Your sister did sustain some serious injuries, Doreen. We got her stabilized and right now she's in surgery."

"Will she be okay?" Fresh tears fell and she dabbed at them with the tissue she clutched.

"There's internal bleeding, but we don't know yet how much damage there is. A neurosurgeon will check the extent of her head injuries. Right now, there's concern about pressure building up in her skull. Linda's other injury was a compound fracture of her left leg. The orthopedic surgeon will likely have to put a rod in to stabilize it, but that will be done when the other issues are under control. Once she's done, the doctors will transfer her to Recovery and then ICU."

"Oh my God. I don't know where to begin. Can I see her?"

"You'll be able to see her once they have her settled upstairs. I'm sure she'll be glad to have you with her when she wakes up, Doreen."

"If only she had listened to us. My mother and sisters have been after her for years to leave that piece of shit. Sometimes I just wanted to drag her away from there, but she always went back, insisting he loved her. Saying we just didn't understand him the way she did. Bastard."

"Linda will need your support now more than ever. I can see your concern for her." Nydia covered Doreen's hands with her own for a moment and let go. "Keep remembering that she is alive and here with you now. She'll recover, but only with help. That's what you need to focus on."

"Thank you so much for what you've done for her, Dr. Rogers. I'll never be able to thank you for saving her. I'm sorry I lost my temper. I'm just so frustrated."

"I understand. It's always hard to fight for people when they don't want you to. In the meantime, I'll send one of the orderlies to take you upstairs to wait, and you can speak to her surgeon when he's through."

Nydia stood up, but before she could leave Doreen rose and enclosed her in a hug. Nydia returned the hug, trying to offer what little support she could. Once Doreen let go, Nydia walked out, the door softly closing behind her.

As Nydia passed the visitor area on her way to the nurses' station to finish her paperwork on Linda, she heard raised voices coming from inside. The view was blocked by a small wall that also caused the voices to be muffled, but since she could hear the voices, they had to be loud and angry by what she could make out.

"Exactly what I need right now." However, as she sat down and began to input her patient information into the computer, she couldn't help but make out bits and pieces of the argument.

She turned to Janet, the nurse sitting next to her. "Anything we need to call security about?"

"No, I don't think so. I walked by a moment ago and saw a uniformed officer arguing with, I think, a detective."

"Reason enough to ignore the idiots," Nydia muttered as she glanced over her shoulder at the wall and then looked back at her work.

The voices got louder. "I don't care what you want," the stifled sound of a female voice said.

A male voice responded louder. "What I want is this collar. My partner and I earned it. If that bitch dies, we get manslaughter. As it stands, we've got attempted charges. That will get me one step closer to detective."

"First you have to explain how the guy broke his arm and why you were inside with no backup."

"I don't have to explain shit to you or anyone, and you know it. The only thing that matters is who you know, and we all know I got that covered."

Nydia glanced toward the wall. "Typical. The only things cops care about are their own asses and how to get ahead of the game," Nydia muttered as she tried to focus on her work. However, the pair soon caught Nydia's attention again.

"Listen, you don't get the collar and you better hope the suspect doesn't press charges. No one in my unit is going to back you and your partner up on any lame ass story you come up with."

"Fuck you."

After signing off on the chart, Nydia spun her chair around, grabbed a clipboard, and stood up, only to crash into someone who had walked up beside her.

"I'm sorry," she said looking down at the clipboard she'd dropped.

"No, it was my fault. I shouldn't have been standing so close," a woman said as she bent to pick it up.

The woman stood up and Nydia came face to face with Jo Powers. For a brief moment, Nydia smiled, glad to see her again. Then she remembered the argument and realized that since she was leaving the room, Jo was the woman she heard. The way Jo stood up to her fellow cop was unexpected, and Nydia wasn't sure what to make of the situation. *Was she sincere? But would she go so far as to turn him in? I would like to think so, but in reality, probably not."*

Jo touched her forearm. "Are you okay?"

Nydia smiled as she recalled the easy banter and flirting from their first meeting. When she realized she was staring at Jo's hand, Nydia tried to look away. Instead, her eyes settled on the way the tailored shirt and blazer Jo wore showed off her womanly figure.

Nydia flushed. "Uhm, yeah I'm fine thanks."

She looked down as Jo's hand fell away. A shiver ran up Nydia's spine.

"Well, I just wanted to say thanks for taking such good care of me," Jo said.

Nydia looked up and caught sight of Jo's badge before their eyes met. "No problem, officer. I was doing my job."

Jo's smile disappeared and was replaced with a small frown. Nydia had a twinge of sadness as she realized she was the cause, but she pushed the feeling down.

Jo's body language became stiff and made her appear sad. "Even so, I really appreciated it."

"Well, I was glad to help, Officer Powers."

"Detective. How is the woman who was brought in? The assault victim?"

Nydia noticed Jo scuffing the toe of her shoe on the floor in a nervous fashion and thought, *she hadn't struck me as someone who got nervous easily. I wonder what's up with that.* She looked at Jo as she said, "Oh, yes, thanks for reminding me. I'm supposed to go over everything with the new head IPV Unit officer. I almost forgot," she said, blushing.

Jo's demeanor changed. "Well, that would be me, so you're in luck. I'm the unit head."

"Oh, the police department isn't exactly well known for its diversity and forward-thinking. I'm surprised they let a woman be in charge. Sorry. Yes, well, she'll be touch and go for the next twenty-four hours. Right now, Linda is up in surgery. We'll have to wait for her to wake up to ascertain any cognitive damage caused by the injuries to her head. Hopefully it will be minimal. If everything goes well over the next few days, I don't foresee too many complications other than infection, with no long-term physical effects."

"Do you have anything as far as evidence goes?" Jo asked.

Nydia's anger rose at the question. Her jaw muscles clenched. "No, I'm sorry, Detective. We were too busy saving her life to have the luxury of time for that. You can take pictures of her injuries when they take her to ICU. Her blood covered clothes are in bags. Check with the supervising trauma nurse if you need anything else."

"Okay, between the pictures, her injuries, and what we recovered at the scene, that should be enough to go on without it. I hope she comes out of surgery all right like you said."

Jo's eyes appeared to lose their sparkle, but for a moment Nydia caught a glimpse of the intelligence and caring within those eyes and felt guilty about her own reaction. Displays of caring emotions weren't something she encountered from the police. Then, again, she usually didn't care enough to consider any of them that close. However, for some reason, when she and Jo interacted, Nydia looked past the badge and saw the attractive, fun woman. She didn't want this meeting to end.

"Uhm, would you like to grab some coffee? I mean if you want to go over the details or something," Nydia asked, going against her usual instincts.

"I'd love nothing more right now."

As Nydia led her to the doctors' lounge, she thought she heard Jo add, "Except to spend time with you." But she couldn't be sure.

However, Nydia couldn't help but shudder at the sound Jo's badge made as she walked. Nydia let out a silent, deep breath, and felt her shoulders release the tension she had been holding. She needed to relax. Jo stepped around her to hold the lounge door open.

"Thank you."

"My pleasure entirely," Jo said with a wink.

Jo Powers has the strangest effect on me. I don't know what this feeling is. It's different, and I'm not sure if that's good or bad. She has me so confused. Maybe conflicted is more the right word. I just don't know anymore.

"Grab a seat. I'll get the coffee." She walked to the counter and pulled the pot off the burner. "How do you take it?" Nydia asked, trying to act casual.

"Milk and a little sugar are fine."

As Nydia poured the coffee, she felt as if Jo's eyes were burning her skin. Nydia placed a coffee in front of Jo and took the seat next to her. "So, what happened? When Linda came in, she was in bad shape."

"Linda Wilkes. We got a call to her house from one of the neighbors. It was the fifth time the police were there in the last year. Each time, Ralph, her boyfriend, had beaten her. But she refused to cooperate, so he was released and we didn't have enough on it to pick him up without her testimony." Jo looked into her coffee cup with a frown. "He was a smart one, left no visible marks. I responded to the call last time and you could read the pain in her eyes. This last time the unit car that answered didn't wait for us. Some hothead went running in there alone, said he found Ralph kicking her with his work boots." Jo let out a deep sigh. "By the time we came on the scene, Ralph was handcuffed with a broken arm, screaming about police brutality, and Linda was lying on the floor bleeding and unconscious. We called in the ambulance, and the rest you know. The pictures we will take of Linda's injuries should match up with the work boots. Hopefully, that will be enough for the DA's office. Ralph left some pretty good impressions on her from what I saw on scene. We'll have that along with the blood all over him."

"I pray that when she wakes up, she'll be willing to testify," Nydia said.

"I'm pretty sure she will. We got a call a month ago and she was close. You could see it in the look in her eyes. I've seen it before in some victims I've dealt with. This will probably push her over the line. At least I hope so."

"Why do it? I mean why work on the IPV Unit? It seems like it never changes. People like Linda just keep going back." Nydia knew it sounded callous, but she couldn't help it. "When I deal with people in the ER, I feel frustrated. The difference is, unlike you, I only have to focus on the injuries, not the person, at least not until later. Even then, once they aren't in the ER anymore, someone else takes over. That's what the social work staff is for. But it's so hard when I know that the large majority of the people I treat will, walk out our front doors and go straight back to their abusers. Sometimes I'm so emotionally tired of it."

"I can understand that. For some, it's hard to deal with every day. I do it for the people who we can save. For every Linda Wilkes that you have to fight for, there are others willing to be saved. I admire those who can take a risk on the unknown and get themselves, and sometimes their kids, out of that situation. They want to make a better life."

Nydia could hear the pride in Jo's voice, her chest puffed out a little bit as she spoke. Nydia was surprised. *A cop doing their job for the right reasons. Could she actually believe in the whole 'To Serve and Protect' crap? Is she someone who's willing to look out for other people, rather than using their power to control everyone else?* She thought. "That's a great thing," she said out loud, more to herself than to Jo.

Jo turned a cute shade of pink at the compliment. "Thank you, but it's just me doing my job and I love it," she said, clearing her throat.

Nydia thought about the answer she got. It seemed honest by the way Jo reacted.

"I'm sure you feel the same about your work. From what I've seen, you have real compassion and skill."

"To be truthful, I'm not as confident about it at all anymore." Nydia gave a deep sigh.

"Why?"

"I'm not sure I know if I still care as much as I used to. There was a time I lived and breathed this job. Helping people was my main concern. The adrenaline rush and solving medical mysteries were great, but underneath it all, I wanted to help people. Now I feel like I care more about all the other aspects of my job rather than the human factor. I'm constantly repairing the damage people do to each other or even themselves. I guess I'm getting a little burnt out, maybe."

Jo looked at her with a surprised expression. "You're not old enough to be burned out."

"Thirty-eight is plenty old enough."

"No way. I think you just need some time to yourself. I bet you have no life outside of here, do you?"

Nydia grinned. "No, not much of one, but that's fine with me. I'm used to it."

"Well, I bet if we fixed that you'd begin to feel better about things. You know what they say about no play." Jo sat up straight in her chair. "I've got the perfect solution."

"What?"

"Bowling."

"Bowling?" Nydia held back a snort of laughter. "What is that going to do? I haven't been bowling since high school."

"Well, there you go. You're going through bowling deprivation."

"Bowling deprivation?" Nydia's eyes grew wide. "You've got to be kidding."

"No. I'm serious. I never kid about bowling. We need to get it back in your soul," Jo said with a broad smile that lit up her face.

"My soul?" Nydia was beginning to enjoy the ridiculousness of the conversation. She smiled and then chuckled. "And how do you propose we do that?"

"Are you working tonight?"

"I get off at seven o'clock. Why?"

"Fine, I'll pick you up here at seven-twenty. We can grab a bite before we go."

"Go where?"

"Pro-Star Lanes, of course. I'm taking you bowling tonight." Jo stood up. Without waiting for a response, she opened the door. "It's a date then. I'll see you soon." She closed the door behind her as she left.

Nydia sat in the lounge in stunned silence. *Did I just agree to go out on a date?* She was still smiling when Trudy walked in.

"Oh, there you are. I need you to take a look at the guy in two."

"What?" Nydia said.

"I said I need you to look at the guy in two. Are you okay?" Trudy asked, raising her eyebrows.

"I think I'm going on a date tonight," Nydia said in a low tone. "With a cop." A lump formed in her throat. She swallowed hard to get it loose as she suddenly remembered what Jo and her job stood for. The panic was already starting. She shook her hands in an attempt to force herself to relax.

"Woo hoo!" Trudy yelled, as she sat down. "So, you finally agreed to go out with tall, dark, and gorgeous."

Nydia looked at her friend in a sense of shock.

"What do you mean, 'finally?' She just asked me. Well, told me really."

"Oh, admit it. You two were eyeing each other from the moment she stepped into this hospital."

"I was not. I told you. I don't date police officers."

"Well, apparently you do now," Trudy said with a smug expression on her face as she got up and walked out.

"Apparently," Nydia said in a soft voice as she looked at the closed door.

Chapter Five

NYDIA SUPPRESSED A YAWN as Jo pulled up to Nydia's house. The house was simple, like most of the things in her life. She liked it that way. Nydia looked toward the front door. Jo's profile reflected in the side window as she thought, *but you, Jo Powers, are anything but.* Nydia turned and met Jo's eyes and blushed. "I had fun tonight. Thank you for thinking of it. It's been a long time since I had such a fun time." Nydia let her mind go and thought something outrageous, *and I think part of that is because you aren't like a typical police officer.* Nydia knew it wouldn't be true if it wasn't Jo.

Jo looked at Nydia with her brows furrowed. "I still don't understand how you managed those scores? I thought you didn't play?'

Nydia smiled. "Oh, you mean the three strikes in a row? Just because I haven't bowled since high school doesn't mean I don't know how. Didn't I mention I was on the school's bowling team, and we were the state champs my senior year?"

Nydia chuckled at the squinty-eyed look Jo gave her when the pins went down for the third time. But then Jo let out a huge unrestrained belly laugh. The sound of it filled Nydia with warmth and feelings she hadn't known since childhood. Thinking about it now, Nydia was sure she had never heard such a wondrous sound before. The laughter was deep, free, and contagious. At the time, she had joined in. It was the first good laugh she'd had in a long time and she felt wonderful. Now, Nydia didn't want the evening to end. She looked at Jo, who seemed to be struggling for something to say. They spoke at the same time.

"I guess this is good—"

"Would you like to come in for—"

Jo let out a slight chuckle, while Nydia blushed. She recovered first. "I...I was going to ask if you would like to come in for some coffee."

Jo smiled. "I'd like that very much. Thanks."

Nydia escorted Jo to the front door. She fumbled in her purse for the key, finally finding it in the front pocket. Nydia's hand was shaking as she tried to put the key in the lock. *Why am I so nervous? Maybe because it's been forever since I've been on a date, much less one with a cop.* After two tries, she got the door open. She turned on the light switch to the front hall as she held the door open for Jo. She was vividly aware of Jo's presence as she brushed by her.

Nydia walked toward the back of the house and the kitchen. The old house wasn't the usual open floor plan most of her friends had. Instead, there were rooms with doorways which made it cozy. She reached for the wall as she got to the kitchen entry and turned on the overhead lights. She sensed Jo following close behind. "Have a seat while I get the coffee going. Don't mind the mess, please."

Jo sat. "I always find a little clutter makes a place a home."

Nydia looked around the room. Unopened mail lay haphazardly on the countertop by the phone, while the day's newspaper was open on the Formica table. As she passed the table, she placed her keys down.

Nydia began making the coffee, got the mugs from the cabinet, the milk and sugar, and placed it on a tray. She then checked in the fridge for something to eat, found some cookies and added them.

"I wish I had the opportunity to see you work a trauma. I bet it looks like a well-orchestrated ballet," Jo said.

"What makes you say that?"

"You move with such fluid motions and purpose. I've noticed it in everything you do, even bowling. It's beautiful to watch. Just like you."

"Thank you." Nydia blushed. She sat down and moved her chair closer to Jo while they waited for the coffee to brew. They sat in companionable silence but every so often, Nydia caught Jo looking at her. W*hy do I feel so comfortable with her? We barely know each other.* Nydia pulled her eyes away from Jo's gaze when the coffee had finished. She got up and put everything together on a tray.

"Let's go into the living room. It'll be more comfortable."

"Sure," Jo stood up. "How about I carry the tray for you? You did the rest."

"That would be wonderful. Thank you." Nydia smiled and handed her the tray.

After entering the living room, Jo set the tray on the coffee table. Nydia handed Jo a mug and they settled on each end of the couch. Nydia leaned back into the cushions facing Jo. "So, tell me about yourself. We've spent the whole night together and I feel like I've barely scratched the surface of learning who Jocasta Powers is."

"Well, first there is the matter of calling me Jo. Only my mother calls me Jocasta. Other than that, there isn't much to tell. You already know about my job."

Nydia cringed a little on the inside at the mention of Jo's work. "No, tell me something about you. For instance, what do you find important in your life?"

"My family is the most important part of my life outside of work. It's my mother, Cassandra, my baby sister, Ellie, and me. We live together over on Peconic Road, on the bayside," she said with a smile.

"What about your dad?" Nydia asked, curious about why there was no mention.

"My mother divorced my father when I was twelve."

Nydia was surprised. Jo's voice was laced with a sound of anger. It made Nydia feel anxious, but she decided to ignore it and let Jo continue. She didn't want to let her own emotions ruin what had been a wonderful night so far.

"The man was a shit. Pardon my language. He abused my mother for years, even sent her to the ER several times."

"I'm so sorry to hear that. You don't have to tell me if you don't want to." Nydia placed her hand over Jo's. Deep down though she hoped Jo wouldn't tell her. Thinking about it made her heart race and brought a tightness to her throat.

"No. I want to. It turned out okay. My mom finally left him after he started on us kids. We lived in a women's shelter for a time. Eventually we got out. Mom was lucky she had found a good job years before. She was a waitress and the family she worked for were nice to all of us. I remember the shelter was the first place I think I got a full night's sleep without hearing fighting or breaking furniture in the other room." Jo let out a deep sigh.

Nydia looked into Jo's eyes over the rim of her mug. Jo's mug sat resting on her leg, forgotten, and getting cold.

"I always thought his behavior contributed to my slight womanizing ways. I've been trying to find someone as strong and confident as my mother. Hopefully, I'll find her someday." She looked into Nydia's eyes again as she lifted her mug to her lips.

"Somehow I don't think there is anything slight about it. I bet you have women falling over you." Nydia chuckled. "Your mom sounds wonderful."

Jo laughed. "You're right she is, and none of the women I've met so far can compete." She stared into her mug for a moment and then tilted her head. "So, tell me about your family. Do they live in the area?"

"Yes," Nydia said without further explanation. She put her hand in her lap and ignored the slight squint Jo made at the curt answer.

"So, are you close?"

"No, not really. I'd rather not talk about it, if you don't mind." Nydia sat up straight. The hand holding her mug shook. Nydia turned and set it on the end table, giving her a moment to hide her eyes from Jo and tried to gather herself.

"How come? Having to deal with life and death every day is what draws me close to mine. I mean, I think in your line of work family would be important. You know, to offer some emotional support."

How dare she? Nydia thought as she turned back, almost knocking the mug over, and glared at Jo, her eyes almost sparking as her face grew hot with anger. "To be honest, Jo, it's none of your damn business. If you could stop being a cop for five minutes, you would've understood that when I said I don't want to talk about it, I don't want to talk about it. My God, you people can be so controlling and domineering. It's as if that's all you know how to do."

"For crying out loud, what does my being a cop have anything to do with it? I just wanted to get to know you better. We didn't talk that much about ourselves tonight. I thought this could be a good chance to get to know each other. I want to learn who you are, Nydia."

Jo's brow wrinkled and she sounded confused, but Nydia didn't care. Right now, all she knew was a simmering rage that bubbled in her chest. Nydia's fury seethed to the top.

"It has everything to do with it. You people never know when to stop playing your power games. Did it even occur to you that it was a closed subject, that maybe, maybe I didn't want to get into it? Of course not. Because you people don't have the common manners or decency, to realize when people don't want to talk to you. You just ignore their wants and needs, and automatically think yours are more important."

"Nydia, I don't understand. That's not what I meant. I thought that if I got you to talk, you might share with me, open up. I get the feeling you don't do that much with people. But I want to get to know you, Nydia, all of you. I have from the moment we met."

"Who I share myself with is of no concern to you. I think you should leave now." Nydia stood up and walked away. As she opened the front door, she turned to see Jo still sitting on the couch, her face full of hurt, her bright smile gone, and her eyes no longer shone. Jo's eyes grew wet with tears, but Nydia ignored it.

"I said I want you to leave, or do I need to call the police and have you forcibly removed?"

Jo walked to Nydia and stood toe to toe with her. "No, you don't need to call the police. I felt a connection to you from the moment I first saw you, and deep down inside I know you felt it too. No matter how much you try to deny it or push it away, it's there."

Jo turned and walked out the door, Nydia closing it behind her. Nydia's vision grew blurry because of the tears in her eyes. She felt hurt and betrayed, but sensed she had let something, and someone, wonderful walk out of her life. Despite that, she refused to let the tears fall. She turned off the lights and leaned her back against the door.

***

Jo blinked away the tears stinging her eyes. She began the drive home with a pain in her chest but got only as far as the end of the street before pulling over. She had no idea how long it took to be able to control her pain, and let it turn to anger. *How could she accuse me of all that? She doesn't know me. Hell, she didn't even give me a chance. Who does she think she is? Why does she affect me so much? I feel like I just lost the most important thing in my life.*

She hit the steering wheel with the palm of her hand. *Why did she get upset when all I did was ask about her family? What was so wrong with that? Maybe it has more to do with her feelings about them than me. I don't understand any of it but do know I can't leave us like this. Nydia is too special to let go. I need to talk to her.*

Jo turned the car around and drove back to the house. She parked and tried to think about what she could do or say. *How can I make her understand?* She strode up the walkway and noticed the downstairs was dark. She started to ring the bell anyway, but something stopped her—the sound of Nydia crying. Jo looked through the frosted sidelight and saw her on the floor. The sight wounded her. *How did we come to be like this? How did I hurt her so badly*?

Jo tapped on the glass. "Nydia, it's Jo. Open the door, please. I want to talk to you." There was no answer. "Please, I can explain everything." Her voice cracked. "I never meant to push you. I would never make you do something you didn't want to. You have to believe me."

Nydia had stopped crying, but Jo could still see her lying on the floor. After a moment, Nydia stood up and Jo's optimism grew. She rested her forehead against the door. "I don't know. Maybe you're right and I've been a cop too long. But I didn't mean to be one with you. I only want to be your friend. Maybe even something more, if you can give me a chance. Please, Nydia, open the door. Let's talk about this. Don't give up on us, I'm begging you."

Jo's shoulders slumped and her body trembled as she waited for a response. Jo hoped with every passing second that Nydia would open the door. Instead, Nydia walked up the stairs.

"Nydia, don't do this." Jo called. "I'm not leaving. I'll stay right here until you talk to me. Please, Nydia. Please." She watched as Nydia stopped at the top for a moment, but then kept going.

Jo saw the light upstairs come on, and, after a minute, go off. She hit the doorjamb with the palm of her hand, while tears started to fall. Jo went to the porch swing at the end of the porch and sat down to think of what to do next. She wouldn't leave that was for sure. She couldn't. Her heart told her too much was at stake.

Chapter Six

NYDIA WOKE FROM A fitful sleep. It wasn't until the early morning hours that exhaustion led to slumber. The night's dreams were full of loss, pain, anger, and hurt-filled piercing blue eyes. As she got into the shower and the water hit her tense body, her mind turned back to the events of the previous evening. *What did I do? She didn't deserve the stuff I threw at her. Can I blame my own demons on her? Is it really fair?* Nydia's chest tightened, overcome with regret and a sense of loss, as she remembered Jo begging her to open the door.

I just don't think I'm strong enough to give anyone my heart, especially not someone like Jo. I'm too damaged for anyone. As she got dressed, she decided she didn't have the stomach for breakfast. Coffee at the Mini-Mart would have to suffice. She went downstairs and grabbed her keys and wallet off the kitchen table.

Nydia stepped outside and was shocked to see Jo's car parked at the curb. *Did she sleep in her car? Oh God, I will feel so bad if she did. But why would she? I know she said she would stay, but that was only to get me to open the door. She didn't mean I, right?*

The sound of a faint snore caught her attention. There on the swing was Jo curled up and asleep, her jacket over her as a makeshift blanket.

Nydia sighed. While the weather had been nice overnight, the humidity mixed with the cool overnight air created a layer of dew and now Jo, her hair wet, shivered in her sleep.

The detective was beautiful, even snoring. She walked over to Jo and knelt beside her. *What does she see in me? I'm a plain, insignificant person with one good friend and that's it. I don't have the ability to let a pet in my life let alone a person. Jo scares me.* She couldn't help the stirring of desire that welled up in her. Given half a chance, she knew she could easily have deep feelings for Jo. But she knew her mind would never let her heart overrule the fear and anger she held inside. Nydia couldn't imagine a force that would. The best thing for both of them was for this to stop, whatever "this" was.

***

Something touched Jo's shoulder. She grabbed it as she tried to stand up, but her legs were entangled. She fell, but instead of landing on the ground found herself on a soft body. She opened her eyes and saw Nydia's eyes filling with tears. With a soft caress, she wiped them away.

Nydia jerked her head and tried to move away. "Uhm, you can get off now."

The moment broken, Jo's heart felt pain. "Yeah, sorry." Jo stood and held out a hand to help Nydia up. Nydia hesitated before taking it. Her hand in Jo's felt right to Jo, and her world narrowed to this instant and the connection she sensed between them. Jo saw goosebumps rise on Nydia's arm. *I think she feels this too. But why is she pushing me away? Why try so hard to hate someone? I'm not giving up. I'll have to work harder to prove myself to her.*

"You need to go home, Jo. There's nothing here for you," Nydia said in a strangled voice.

Jo knew she was lying when Nydia averted her gaze, and yet still held Jo's hand. "No, not until we talk about this. I can see it in your eyes, and I feel it in your touch."

Nydia looked at their joined hands and pulled hers away with such force that Jo almost lost her balance again.

"We need to talk this out, for both our sakes. You know in your heart I'm right," Jo said, pleading with everything she had, her voice cracking with emotion.

"No. There's nothing to talk about. I can't do it. I won't get involved with a cop, not any cop. I'm just not strong enough. Last night proved that."

"Í know it's a dangerous job, Nydia, but—"

"It's not that. It's who you are, what you are. I know all about you. Your need for control, the sense of superiority, the power you relish having. It's all a part of you. You can't help but use it every chance you get. I know from experience. Cops do nothing but abuse people and control them for their own benefit."

Jo was stunned into silence. She didn't know how to respond, and her chest grew painful and tight. *Is this how she really feels about me? Does she think so little of me? No. I refuse to believe that.*

Jo squared her shoulders. "But you don't know me. I'm not like that. Just give me a chance to prove it to you. I became a cop because I wanted to protect people, not abuse them. I would never dream of using my authority against someone. I swear. Give me the chance to show you who I am. Believe me, and in me." Jo's heart beat faster. "I'm worth it. We're worth it." She almost stuttered trying to get the words out fast enough for Nydia to listen before it was too late.

"I don't think I can do that, Jo. I'm just not strong enough." Nydia's shoulders slumped as she looked down.

Jo reached out her hand, placed it under Nydia's chin, and lifted her head so she could look into Jo's eyes. "We can be strong together. I'll be there with you. I want to be with you, Nydia. We can do this. Please don't throw it away before we even have a chance to start."

Jo couldn't take it anymore as tears began to run down Nydia's face. She took her in her arms and hugged her until Nydia sniffled and wiped her eyes on Jo's shoulder. She took the risk and again placed her hand under Nydia's chin and lifted her face. This time, she bent and gently placed a kiss on Nydia's lips. It wasn't a kiss of passion, but one of comfort, hope, and tenderness. With it, she let Nydia know she would take care of her heart.

Nydia stiffened, but then instead of pulling away, she leaned further into Jo and began kissing her back. Jo rejoiced in the taste of Nydia's lips and sensed something strong pass between them. She hoped Nydia experienced it as well.

Nydia pulled back. "What you make me feel, Jo, confuses me. When I'm in your arms, I feel safe for the first time in years. I feel at home in spite of everything. But I also know your job is who you are, and despite that, I want to be with you." Nydia moved closer, wrapped her arms around her, and rested her cheek on Jo's shoulder. Nydia took a deep breath and let it out. "I still don't know if I can do this, Jo. I feel so lost."

Jo felt relieved as Nydia relaxed into her. "You can, Nydia. I know you're strong enough. I can feel it. What we have is too special for you to give up on without a chance. We will fight for it together." Jo placed a gentle kiss on the crown of Nydia's head. "Come on. Let me take you to work. You're in no shape to drive right now."

"Okay, come inside and I'll get you some coffee before we go. Maybe you can warm up a little."

"I don't need anything but you right now," Jo said, as she led Nydia to the car.

***

Jo pulled the car to a stop outside the Emergency Room entrance. Nydia spent most of the drive examining Jo's profile. The soft strength it held captivated her. *Can I ever be worthy of someone like her*?

"You've been quiet," Jo said as she turned toward Nydia. "Would you rather not go to work?"

Nydia was touched by the concern she heard, and Jo's eyes and face softened. *Her empathy shines through everything she does. I'll have to find my strength in her for now. If she is willing to believe in us, I will too.* She took hold of Jo's hand and intertwined their fingers as if it was the most natural thing in the world to do.

"No, I'll be fine. I need time, that's all. This feels so fast. It's taken me by surprise. I hope you understand." She looked away. "When will I see you again?"

"I do. I assumed I would pick you up, so I'll be here when you get off. We can talk some more tonight if you want. If it's too much, you can give me your keys and I can arrange for your car to be here." Jo squeezed Nydia's hand before letting it go.

Nydia blushed. "Then I'll see you later."

She let out a sigh when Jo's soft lips touched hers. The feeling she got was like nothing she recalled—it was warm, and safe, and filled with promises of more, and yet it was also gentle. The emotions reached her core and were something she hoped to hold onto all day.

"I don't know why, but kissing you feels so right," Jo said.

Nydia smiled at her and closed her eyes halfway. "Thanks. I think I really needed that right now."

"Happy to oblige, anytime. Let me know whenever you need another. Believe me, I have my own selfish reasons for giving them."

"I will." A bright smile reflected Nydia's sudden sense of confidence as she got out of the car. She waved before going through the ER door.

Chapter Seven

NYDIA COULDN'T REMEMBER A time when she had been so exhilarated. She had her good and bad days the same as everyone, but she had a steady dose of joy and happiness going over the last few months. *Not since I was a kid and mom was here. I can't say how long it's been since I felt so free and cared for.*

Nydia was drawn out of her thoughts by the beeping of a car horn. She welcomed the sight of Jo resting her arm on the car door through the open window. She stood up from the porch swing and walked over.

Jo smiled. "Care for a lift, little girl?"

Nydia grinned. "I don't know, can you be trusted?"

Jo reached out and took hold of Nydia's hand. "Always."

"I believe you."

Jo smiled again and tapped the windowsill with the palm of her hand. "Good. I had some candy to offer, but I'll keep it for next time."

Nydia laughed as she walked around to the passenger side and got in. "I bet you do, along with a trench coat."

"Nah. The candy is as far as I'll go. The coat is too cliché." Jo started the car. "So, are you ready for our grand adventure?"

"Sure. Once you tell me what it is."

"Fine, be that way and spoil it."

Nydia playfully slapped Jo on the shoulder. "Spoil what? You're going to have to tell me at some point."

Jo pulled away from the curb. "Well, with your permission of course, I was thinking a drive out to Orient Point. We could do lunch at the restaurant by the water while we watch the ferries come and go. Then perhaps a walk in the park along the water. If that doesn't appeal to you, we can do a winery crawl. The sunshine should make for a nice picnic. We could stop off at Love Lane and pick up some food at the market."

Nydia relaxed into the seat as she put on her sunglasses. "I think a drive and lunch sounds like a great way to spend the day. I still can't believe summer is almost over."

"I know. It feels like time has been flying by. Especially these last three months." Jo grinned. "I know our schedules are both busy, but I'm glad we've been able to get together as much as we can, and talk on the phone and Facetime when we can't."

Nydia smiled. "Yes, I've liked that."

"With summer ending, I hope we can free up more time to enjoy together. Less day to day city-idiots to get into trouble all day."

"I do too. Of course, we still have to contend with pumpkin season. Lucky for me it slows down to basic fender-benders and light injuries. Though there are the odd farming accidents."

"Yeah, it will be nice. I hate to say it, but even though we've been dating for so long, I feel like it's still so new."

"I know what you mean. But slow has been good. I think it's what I needed to feel comfortable." Nydia said. "It's been forever since I've tried for a relationship with someone."

"So, you've mentioned. I still don't know how I got to be the lucky one, but I'm happy I am."

"You got lucky because you are you. You're kind, understanding, and have a beautiful soul. I haven't had much experience with someone like you." Nydia's smile became a frown and she turned to look out at the passing scenery.

Without taking her eyes off the road, Jo reached over and placed her hand on Nydia's thigh. "Hey, are you okay?"

"Maybe. I'm being melancholy is all, wondering how I managed to keep you this long."

"You need to stop thinking so little of yourself, and us. I don't know what happened in your past, and I hope someday you'll feel able to share that part of yourself with me. Until then, though, I feel like I've won the lottery in the fact that you've let me into your life." Jo took Nydia's hand in hers and brought it to her lips. She placed a soft kiss on the palm and rested their joined hands on her chest. "For now, let's just enjoy the day."

"Sounds like a wonderful idea." Nydia smiled and pulled their hands onto her lap. "When we're together sometimes I feel like I could have a whole new start with you, Jo Powers."

Jo smiled the largest smile Nydia had seen on her yet. "I hope you can."

Chapter Eight

AS THE SEASON PASSED into fall, Jo and Nydia had gotten into a new routine. In early October, Nydia sat upstairs putting on her shoes. She smiled when she heard the front door open and close. *For the first time since I can recall, I actually enjoy my life. I have a reason to wake up every morning other than work.* She rushed downstairs and found Jo standing at the kitchen sink filling the teakettle. Nydia came up behind her and wrapped her arms around Jo's waist.

"I enjoy this new habit of ours."

Jo turned around, leaned in, and kissed Nydia gently on the lips. "I do too. Thank you for thinking of it and then trusting me enough to give me a key to your home."

"I decided if we couldn't find time after work, we might have a better chance beforehand."

"And you were right. I enjoy starting out my day over breakfast with you. Let me put the water on for your tea, and then get my coffee going. So, what's for breakfast today?"

Nydia let go and watched as Jo turned and put the electric kettle down on its base, hit the switch, and grabbed the coffee pot. "I was thinking omelets. Do you want cheese or western?" Nydia walked over to the stove and turned it to low.

"Western sounds good."

"I was hoping you would say that. I have everything prepared. I got home late and wasn't ready for bed, yet, so I chopped vegetables and puttered around for a while."

Jo frowned. "You should have called me."

"It was late. Too late to bother you, since I knew I would be seeing you. You get up early for this."

Jo came over to Nydia, and pointed between them. "This, here, is something I want to do and enjoy, and I would have enjoyed time on the phone with you last night too. So, never hesitate to call." Jo tapped the tip of Nydia's nose. "Ever."

Nydia considered Jo's statement and thought, *Wow, what did I ever do to deserve you? I'm afraid you're a dream sometimes.* Nydia let out a sigh before she replied to Jo. "I won't. I promise, but if I keep you up late you have my okay to skip coming over."

"The only way I'm missing this, is if I'm lying sick in bed. Oh, then you can stop by and play 'doctor'".

Nydia blushed and looked away.

"Hey, I was teasing. We agreed to go slow with this relationship, and we will. We do things when you're ready. I don't want you to think I'm pressuring you. I'm not, and never would."

"I know you wouldn't, and I thank you for being willing to take it at such a slow pace. I guess I was feeling a bit self-conscious for a second."

"Well, you have no reason to be. So, no more worrying and let's have some of your wonderful omelets."

Nydia wasn't the least bit surprised when Jo finished her statement off with a kiss, one Nydia was glad to return.

***

Jo stopped her car by the hospital ER entrance. They took turns driving each other to work, so today Nydia got to sit and admire Jo as she drove. After putting the car in park, Jo turned and said, "Remember to take your lunch."

Nydia held up the brown paper bag. "Got it right here."

"And play well with the other kids at recess."

"I promise." Nydia laughed.

"Okay, as long as you promise. Now, give me a kiss before you run off on me."

Nydia leaned over the console and ran her hand up the side of Jo's neck. When she reached Jo's jawline, she drew a finger along it from her ear to her chin. Crooking her finger under it she pulled Jo forward. "You want a kiss?"

"Uhm..."

"Do you need one to last until tomorrow?" Nydia kissed Jo before Jo had a chance to gather a thought. It was a long, deep kiss that left them both breathless.

When Nydia pulled back, Jo had a grin from ear to ear. "Yeah that'll keep me, I think."

"Good. I'm glad I could accommodate you. Come back soon and I'll see what I can do to replenish you." Nydia said and smiled back.

Nydia turned to get out of the car and saw Trudy looking at them through the glass of the ER doors. Nydia was unable to contain her happiness. She hadn't told Trudy about her mornings with Jo, so she was sure she was in for an inquisition once she got inside. But right now, she didn't care. She chuckled at the idea and stepped out of the car. As she neared the door, a painful grip landed on her arm and made her spin around. She came face to face with Dr. Goddard.

"You heathen. I can't believe you would bring such evilness here and flaunt it in front of the hospital. Anyone could have seen you. It's bad enough they let people like you work here and interact with patients, but to carry on in such a sinful manner is beyond acceptable. I'm going to speak to Dr. Stephenson about this."

Before Nydia had a chance to respond, he let go. Nydia was stunned for a moment but came out of it to realize that he had let go. She saw Dr. Goddard had an arm held behind his back, and behind him, she saw a six-foot tall angry woman holding him by the arm and the scruff of his shirt. The furious doctor's veins were standing out in his neck, and his face was red with anger. He stood on the tips of his toes trying to relieve the pressure.

"Let go of me, you piece of filth," he said as he tried to pull away from Jo. "Do you have any idea who you're dealing with?"

"No, I don't and I don't really care. However, you might." Jo shoved her badge under his nose.

"I know they've been forced to let women into the police department, but to allow people like you is disgusting. What kind of sick society are we living in?" Dr. Goddard's words of anger and disgust oozed off him as if they were physical.

"The kind that allows for civil rights. Something a moron such as yourself wouldn't understand," Jo said, shaking him.

Nydia felt her anxiety climb as her old fears began to rise. "Jo, please don't do this."

"If you ever touch her again, I will make sure you have limited use of this arm."

Nydia's voice rose. "Jo, please, I'm begging you. You're scaring me."

Jo stared at Nydia for a moment, and then she looked between her and Dr. Goddard. Jo's angry demeanor disappeared, and with one last jostle, Jo let the doctor go with a slight shove.

"I'll have both your jobs for this. How dare you treat upstanding citizens like this. As for you, Nydia, I will have you up before the Board." Dr. Goddard turned and stormed into the hospital.

Jo's body seemed to have lost all its steam. She bent her head and her shoulders were slumped. "I'm sorry. I never should have done that. It's just that when I saw him grab you, I thought he was going to hurt you. Nothing would wound me more than to see you hurt." Jo looked into Nydia's eyes.

Nydia's conflicting emotions tore at her. She was afraid that all her worries were coming true. However, she watched as the woman who was quickly becoming her strength crumbled in front of her. Nydia's decision was made when she saw the look of loss in Jo's eyes. "It's okay, Jo. But please don't let it happen again. I hate to think of you that way."

"I promise you it will never happen again. Please believe me. But it was reflex when I saw him grab you."

"I believe you, Jo. But it's those reflexes that scare me. You don't seem to realize the power you hold over people. You can't do that to someone because it's easy, or you're able to. Otherwise, you're like the rest of them...someone who throws their ability to control others around with a disregard for anyone else."

"I'm sorry. I swear that's not who I am. Not by a long shot. I hope someday you'll trust me fully so that you can find it in you to share with me why you feel this way. I want to understand and know every part of you." Jo opened her arms.

Nydia did not resist as Jo engulfed her in a long, deep hug. She felt safe in Jo's arms. After several moments, Jo placed a tender kiss on her lips. The kiss lingered longer than the previous one and wasn't as deep and longing, but it felt gentle and reassuring to her.

Nydia sighed. "Thank you."

"You better get inside, otherwise I'll stay and make you late."

"You're right, I should. But you're not making this easy for me." Nydia leaned back in Jo's arms.

"Okay, you win this time." Jo let go of her. "I'll see you at seven."

A shiver ran up Nydia's spine at the thought of losing Jo. A feeling of emptiness—but she ignored it. She didn't want to contemplate it. "It's a date then."

Jo cupped Nydia's cheek and placed a kiss on her forehead. "It's definitely a date." She rewarded Jo with a bright smile. "I'll carry that look with me the rest of the day."

Nydia watched Jo walk away, admiring her physique. The strength she had showed in her walk and stature. Her wide shoulders, firm thighs, and muscled arms, combined with her swagger, let everyone who met her know she could back up her words with action.

After she watched Jo get back in her car, Nydia went into the ER. Entering the doctors' lounge, she saw Trudy sitting at the break table looking at some papers. Nydia noticed the paper was upside down.

"Good morning, Trudy," Nydia said, as she snagged a doughnut out of the box on the counter and turned around.

"Good morning to you too. Can I guess the smile on your face has something to do with the little display I saw outside? Or does it have more to do with the raging scowl Dr. Goddard gave me as he went by?"

"Why yes, it does have to do with the lovely woman who dropped me off, as you well know since you were spying. Dr. Goddard is a side benefit. I can't believe he had the gall to do that."

"I saw part of that before running back here and looking uninterested. Jo had it well under control from what I saw."

"You failed on the last part." Nydia was still a bit rattled by Dr. Goddard and Jo's reaction. For now, she just wanted to focus on the morning before all of that. Nydia smiled remembering the kiss in the car.

"So, what about Goddard? What did you do to him to cause Jo to lay hands to him?"

Nydia took a quick bite of her doughnut. "Oh, him? He took offense to my 'lifestyle choices,' again."

"Calling it that is being kind to him, as I'm sure he used worse than that."

Nydia let out a deep sigh. "You're right. Nothing new there. However, this time he got a little on the touchy side trying to express his viewpoint."

"Ah, that would explain Jo's reaction and the vein sticking out on his forehead when he strode past here. I figured he did something to have her put him in an arm lock. I think Janet may have seen it go down."

"An audience is not what I needed, crap."

"Be careful, Nydia. I saw him heading into Dr. Stephenson's office."

"Oh, geez, that could be a problem, but let's hope not. Either way, I have too many good things going on in my life right now to worry about his petty behavior."

"Okay. Whatever you say. You're the doctor."

"Speaking of being a doctor, let's go get a chart so I can start working," Nydia said as they walked out of the lounge and headed toward the nurses' station.

Going around the desk Trudy handed Nydia one of the patient tablets. "Here you go. Something nice and easy to start your day."

"Why does your idea of easy make me nervous?" Nydia called over her shoulder as she went into exam room two.

Chapter Nine

NYDIA SAT IN HER office a few hours later, drinking coffee from the Lounge that was thick, sludgy, and tasted burnt. Hospital coffee was one of the main reasons she drank tea off-hours. Her feet rested on the small stool next to her desk. *God this feels good. Well except for the coffee but can't be too choosy*. She put her head back and closed her eyes, hoping to bring up images of a certain dark-haired, blue-eyed detective. Instead, the door in front of her opened, disturbing her solitude.

Annoyed at the interruption, and that someone came in without knocking, she was ready to let loose, but stopped when she saw Jim standing by the door. Her irritation disappeared and her stomach dropped and she sat up straight.

"Hello, Jim. What can I help you with?"

"Sorry to barge in Nydia, but you left the door ajar. I didn't realize you were resting." Jim sat down across from her and looked at her with a worried expression.

"No problem, Jim. You're allowed to come in anytime."

"Well, either way, I hate to disturb your break, but I had a visit from Dr. Goddard earlier."

Nydia put her coffee down. "Oh."

"Yes, I imagine you have an idea about what he had to say."

Nydia picked up her mug again, and took a sip to hide her worry. "I have an idea it wasn't anything praiseworthy."

Jim chuckled, "No, it never is. Is it?" He walked over to the chair on the other side of the desk, moved the pile of journals onto the floor, and sat down. "This should be more official, but I wanted to give you a chance to have your say before I go further and handle this. According to Dr. Goddard you 'defiled the reputation of the hospital, committed violations of morality, and had him assaulted.' I'm going to guess there's more to it."

"How is the jury leaning?" Nydia set her mug on the desk and leaned forward.

"My leaning is that Dr. Goddard is a close-minded bigot with an egocentric, adolescent mentality."

"But—" she said, knowing there must be more to come.

"But his complaint is official, so it will have to be reviewed by me and, if necessary, the Board. So far, I see no reason to involve the Board as long as you can tell me what really happened. Because I'm almost sure his version is a bit embellished."

"Well, I'm seeing someone. They drove me to work this morning. As we were saying goodbye in the car, Dr. Goddard must have seen us. He took offense."

"Why would he do that? What goes on in your car is between you and the person in question, not Dr. Goddard."

Nydia took a deep breath and her palms were sweaty. She had never considered it necessary to share her personal life with her boss. Why bring it up? She hadn't dated much, and certainly not anyone from work. Trudy was the only one who knew. *You can do this. You owe it to yourself and Jo.*

"It was a her."

"Okay."

Nydia raised her eyebrows.

"I didn't think you kept your sexual orientation a secret. Was I mistaken?"

"I try to keep my personal life private, but I didn't know that you knew it."

"Of course, I did. I've known you a long time, Nydia. I would like to think we've become close over those years." Jim leaned back in his chair. "So, what happened after he saw you?"

"As I headed into work, he grabbed my arm. He started spouting about perversion, morality, and the good reputation of the hospital being smeared. He was quite aggressive in expressing his beliefs."

"He grabbed you?" Jim leaned forward again. "Did he hurt you?"

"Not really. I just have a little bruising, that's all."

"He grabbed you hard enough to bruise you?"

"It all happened so fast. But, yes."

"It would help if someone witnessed it. Did anyone?"

"Nurse Swenson, at least most of it I'm sure. I expect you can get a statement from her. She told me one of the other nurses was outside at the time. You can ask her for the details."

"I will. So, then what happened? Dr. Goddard said you had him assaulted. I'm going to assume there's more to it than that as well."

"Yes, there is. When he grabbed me, my friend got out of the car and pulled him off. She's a police detective and was worried about me. I know she may have been too physical with him. I'm sorry if it's caused you trouble, Jim. If you need to take any action, I understand."

Jim raised an eyebrow. "Why would I do that? It sounds to me that he should be the one brought up on charges. I should have him before the Board. But I'm going to let you choose whether to press charges or not. It's your department and your staff."

Nydia was quiet for a few moments, her brows furrowed. "Thank you, Jim. I want to make sure there's a written statement on the record, but in the end, I'm just glad you believe me."

"I've known you long enough to trust your honesty. I'll have Sara draft something for you to sign. If anything is missing, let me know."

"Thank you. Your opinion means a lot to me, on a personal level, as well as professionally." Nydia began to relax. She hadn't even realized how tense she had become until she felt the muscles in her shoulders release. She handled life and death situations every day with no problem, but this had her stomach in knots.

"Yes, well, it's my pleasure. I only wish I could do more. So, I'll let you get back to work now. I know how busy you get down here. I'm not so old I don't remember my time in the trenches."

As if the ER gods had been listening, her pager went off as a call came over the PA system. "Trauma team to trauma room one."

"Well, I guess my break is over. Thanks again, Jim, for being so understanding." She held out her hand as they stood to leave.

"There was never a real doubt in my mind about you, Nydia. You better get going," he said as they shook hands.

Nydia hurried to the trauma room. She held out her arms for the gloves and gown held by a team member. "What do we have coming in?" she asked Trudy who was standing by the trauma cart looking over its inventory.

"A probable assault victim, according to the EMTs who called it in. They should be here any second."

Before Trudy had a chance to relay any more information, the EMTs pushed a stretcher into the room. Nydia saw Jo beside the stretcher, holding the hand of the patient. Nydia gave Jo a quick glance as she moved closer to the stretcher to see the patient. She was probably late thirties, and bruised, it seemed, from head to toe. Her shirt was barely hanging on since the EMTs had torn it to attach the leads for the monitor. Her jaw and right eye were swollen, her eye almost closed.

The paramedics put an air cast over her left arm and leg in the field. The patient's head was immobilized, and her neck was in a cervical collar. Blood dripped from a scalp wound that the EMTs had put a pressure bandage on, but the blood had already soaked through.

After the EMTs helped transfer the patient to the table, one of them began to rattle off the rest of her medical details. As he did, the team moved in as one.

"All right, people, let's get another IV with saline started and I want X-rays of the leg and arm, and then a CT-scan of the head and neck." Nydia bent over the patient, close to her head. "Hi, I'm Dr. Rogers. I'll be your doctor. Can you tell me your name?"

Nydia spared a glance at Jo as she spoke to the woman. Jo was focused on the patient, ignoring the activity around her. Her smile for the patient didn't reach her eyes. A cold hardness replaced the sparkle that Nydia was used to.

The patient mumbled something that Nydia couldn't make out. She examined the patient's jaw along the bone and up to her ears. "Okay, honey, don't try to talk. I'll be right back after I have a word with the detective who came in with you. All right? Blink once to let me know you understand."

The woman blinked her good eye once, long and slow. Nydia could tell by the way her face tensed and then relaxed, that it took all her energy and concentration even for such a small effort. It worried her enough that she took out her penlight.

"I'm just going to check your eyes. If it hurts, let me know. You can squeeze the detective's hand." Nydia shined the light in each eye, being cautious of the swelling, and saw that her right pupil was slow to respond. "What's her BP again?"

"It's 135 over 82," Janet said as she checked the monitor.

"Okay, let me know right away if anything changes. I'm stepping outside for a minute." Nydia nodded at Jo to follow her out.

The patient refused to let go of Jo's hand. Jo leaned over so the patient could look into her eyes. "I'm only going to be outside. I promise you'll be okay. The nurses will take good care of you and I'll come back as soon as I can." As the woman let go, Janet, one of the nurses, took Jo's spot.

Once she and Jo were outside the room, Nydia asked, "Can you tell me what happened?"

"We got a call from the neighbor saying the husband and wife were having a loud fight, and that it sounded physical. She could hear the wife screaming for help. By the time we got there the husband was gone."

"Was she able to tell you anything?"

"Not much. Based on the condition we found her in and the scene, she may have been sexually assaulted."

Nydia frowned and ran her fingers through her hair. "So, a possible rape."

"Yeah, it looks that way."

"Okay, let me get back in there." As she started back into the room, Nydia realized Jo was following her. "I'm sorry, Jo, but until we get her checked out, I can't let you in. What's her name?"

"Barbara Donnelly."

"Donnelly? That name sounds familiar."

"Do you recognize her?"

"No, but the name sounds familiar." Nydia placed her hand on the door, but Jo laid her hand on Nydia's.

"Can't you let me be there for her? She's hurt and scared, and she has no one right now."

"I know you want to be there for her, but I can't. Procedure is key if you want the husband. You should know that, Jo. Trudy and I will get what evidence we can. We're trained for it, but it has to be done this way."

"I trust you. I only wanted to give her some support, but I'll stay out here." Jo stood up straighter and let go of Nydia. "Can you let her know?"

Nydia took Jo's hand in hers. "Yes. I promise to take care of her."

"I know you will."

Nydia released Jo's hand and went into the room.

***

Barbara Donnelly was rolled back into the trauma room after her CT scan. Nydia followed. Barbara's jaw was bruised down to the bone, but it wasn't broken. Nydia was relieved. She needed a little more information before she could consider it safe to proceed with the rest of the exam.

"Okay, everyone stop what you're doing." Everyone stepped back from the patient. "Mark, is the patient stable?"

"Yes. We administered the pain meds you ordered, and Neurology looked at the scans and cleared her for the time being. Her vitals are holding steady, and Ortho is waiting for your okay. They have the X-rays and said she should be able to wait until you're done."

"Okay then, I want everyone out of here except Trudy."

Several of the staff left, but a few stood and stared at her looking confused.

"I said everyone. What part of that didn't you understand, people?" Nydia asked.

The stragglers scrambled out of the room.

"So, are we ready?" Trudy asked out of earshot of their patient.

"Yes. Did you stay with her the entire time?"

"I never left her except for the CT scan, and then she was within my eyesight. No one touched her except me and the tech."

"I'm going to talk to her. Can you get the Sexual Assault Evidence Kit ready?"

"Sure."

Nydia rolled a stool near the bed and spoke in a calm, gentle voice. "Barbara? I understand the police think you may have been sexually assaulted."

A tear fell from Barbara's eyes. While her heart hurt for Barbara, Nydia's professionalism wouldn't let that stand in the way. If it were her, she would want her partner brought to justice.

Barbara tried to speak. The strain of the movement showed on her face.

Nydia laid her hand on the woman's arm. "No, don't try to speak. I just want you to blink once for yes and two for no, all right?"

Barbara blinked once.

"Okay. Now, I'm going to tell you what we are going to be doing. Trudy," she said pointing to her friend, "is going to be doing what we call a SAEK kit. It will let us gather any evidence of the assault there is. Once she is done with that, I'll do a physical examination, which will include a pelvic exam. Do you understand?"

Barbara blinked again. Her hand hung over the rail.

Nydia reached out and laid her hand on Barbara's. She gave it a soft squeeze. "I know this is scary and uncomfortable for you, but if we can do this, then we can hold him responsible. Do we have your permission to start?"

Once more Barbara blinked.

With a nod from Nydia, Trudy began the forensic exam.

"I need to ask you some questions. Some of them will be awkward and uncomfortable, but I need to ask them. Are you ready?"

Barbara took in a deep breath. After she let it out, she blinked once.

While Nydia asked her questions, Trudy began the process of gathering evidence. Nydia had to move out of the way several times, but otherwise she stayed by Barbara's side.

The only time Barbara faltered was when Trudy was taking a mouth swab. A deep groan escaped from Barbara.

"I'm sorry, honey. I'll give you some more meds for the pain when we're done. Can you hold on a bit more?" Nydia said.

Barbra blinked.

"I'm done," Trudy said in a soft voice as she marked the last of the evidence bags.

"Good. Thanks." It was times like this that Nydia appreciated having Trudy. She was always so tender.

"Barbara, I'm going to start your physical exam. Is that okay?"

Barbara blinked.

"Trudy is going to sit here and keep you company. She'll explain what I'm doing."

Trudy sat down and took Barbara's hand.

Nydia began with the pelvic exam, the most intrusive portion of the exam. "Barbara, you have some tearing and bruising down here so I'm going to take a picture for evidence. Okay?"

Barbara gave a slight nod.

Nydia clicked a few shots, using a ruler next to the marks to show scale. When Nydia finished the exam, she accepted the syringe Trudy handed her and injected the contents into the IV line. "Barbara, we're done. I've given you the pain meds I promised. Try and rest. Sleep if you can."

***

"So, how did it go? Will she be all right?" Jo asked as she stepped into the room after Barbara was rolled out.

"Yeah, eventually," Nydia said as she led Jo out. "Right now, she is battered and bruised, both physically and emotionally. Her arm and wrist and left leg are broken. She has a concussion with a slight fracture, but neurology doesn't think it's severe enough to cause bleeding or swelling. Either way, I am going to keep her here a day or two. That way the social workers will do their jobs, and she'll have a chance to get her emotions under some control. I hope she takes advantage of the local domestic shelters. Trudy has the evidence case ready for us to sign out."

Nydia's shoulders slumped and her eyes were fatigued. She wanted nothing more than for Jo to take her in her arms and lend her some strength, but she knew this was not the place for it.

Jo touched Nydia's arm and backed into one of the curtained exam areas. "Come here. You look tired." Jo said, pulling the curtain closed.

"I am. You make me feel better though. I know you can't fix everything, but you being here helps." Nydia cupped Jo's cheek with her hand. Slowly and gently, she ran her thumb over Jo's silky skin. "You hate these types of calls as much as I do, don't you?"

"Yeah, I do. I think the rape cases like this get to me the most. How could someone who is supposed to love and cherish you, commit such a violent, heinous act? I will never understand it."

Nydia saw the hurt in Jo's eyes and wondered if it was for Jo or her patients. Jo stiffened. Nydia dropped her hand as Jo turned her head.

Dr. Goddard held the curtain that Jo had closed behind them. Nydia watched her. Jo's eyes didn't waver from his, her hands balled into fists and her jaw muscles were clenched. He dropped his gaze, turned, and walked away. Nydia wondered what kind of malevolence he was capable of now since Jo made him look foolish with the confrontation in the parking lot.

Chapter Ten

IT WAS FRIDAY, AND Jo was on edge. She was restless, fidgety, and her patience had gone south. Poor Duncan bore the brunt of it without complaint. Jo was on her way back to her desk with the third cup of coffee of the morning. Like the rest, it would end up sitting and getting cold.

It had been five weeks since her case with Barbara Donnelly opened. Three days after that her morning routine with Nydia had become less frequent. Their schedules kept conflicting. Either one or the other of them had to work late or be in early. One or two days over the last several weekends were all they had.

"I feel like I'm an addict. All I can think about is wrapping my arms around her," Jo said to herself.

"Did you say something?" Duncan asked without taking his eyes off the computer screen.

Jo blushed. "No, I was just thinking out loud." She looked around the station room and noticed that most of the other detectives weren't there. "Where is everyone?"

"Out on calls. Didn't you hear the phones ringing?"

"Oh yeah. The phones. Any more word on the case?"

"What? Which one? We have a few you know." Duncan grimaced as he took a sip of coffee.

"The Donnelly case."

"Ah, well, yes and no. The vic identified the husband and admitted he raped her, but we've had no luck tracking him down. Someone's hiding him. I can feel it."

"Hmm. Where's he been looked for so far?"

"His parent's place, some friends we were able to track down through the wife, and the local dive hotels. We can't find any place he or his family own. He's vanished."

"Do you think he could have friends Barbara doesn't know about?"

"It's possible. She stated he went out a lot to the local bars around the house and near his work. He could know anyone there, the bastard."

"He may be a bastard, but now he's our bastard. Let's go talk to Barbara again. She seemed a bit nervous when we questioned her last time. I don't want to make it worse for her, but maybe we can jog her memory a bit more." Jo stood and grabbed her coat off the back of her chair.

"Right behind you," Duncan said, pulling on his coat.

***

It was six days since she'd last seen Jo, and now Nydia stood in the doctors' lounge alone, staring at the coffee maker trying to will the coffee to come out faster. She turned around when she heard the door open, and was greeted with the sight of Dr. Goddard. *He's looking as sanctimonious as always and as if the stick up his ass has grown a bit.* She turned back to her coffee.

"My day has gone downhill since the moment I walked in this morning, and the kid vomiting on my sneakers was no help. You've barely said a word to me in weeks and you've picked a bad time to start, so, what do you want Dr. Goddard, because I can tell you are about to get on my last nerve?"

"I wanted to let you know that even though you have Dr. Stephenson hoodwinked, Nydia, don't think I won't do everything in my power to see you out of this hospital. I won't let it go. This is not a job for women and especially not women of your ilk. The incident with that woman simply proves you're emotionally and morally unfit for this position, or any position in this hospital," Dr. Goddard said louder than Nydia was going to stand for.

"Yup, I was right. There went my last nerve," she said more to herself than Dr. Goddard. She turned to face him. "First of all, Dr. Goddard, you will address me as Dr. Rogers. I extend the courtesy to you and I expect, and deserve, the same in return—more so, since I am also your supervisor. Second, whether I stay or go has nothing to do with you, thank God, but rather with Dr. Stephenson and the Board. Third, my life, and how I live it, are none of your damn business." Nydia had her hands on her hips, and she was glaring at him. "So, if you're smart, you'll pick your next words very carefully."

Most people she knew would have been smart enough to back off. But he wasn't. His face turned redder, the vein on his forehead became more pronounced, and clenched fists by his side. It was clear he wasn't going to take the hint. *I hope he doesn't get physical again. I'm on my own this time.*

"How dare you talk to me like that? Because someone mistakenly put you in a supervisory role here, does not give you the right to speak to me like this, nor does it give you any respectability. You're lacking both in my eyes. I am a man, a God-fearing Christian, and a husband. Nothing about you or your personal life can compare to that. There isn't one thing about you that is within God's law. The fact that you're spreading your filth by working on patients only sullies the reputation of this hospital, and it is an abomination. God will have no mercy on your soul."

"I don't believe in any God who requires fear to motivate, let's start there," Nydia said. "I believe in a God of love, not vengeance. In addition, women work outside the home now. I know it's a newsflash for you, but please try and keep up with the rest of the world. Again, what I do on my own time has no impact on anyone but me and the person I choose to be with, so stay out of it. How your wife deals with you is beyond me."

"My wife knows her place in life. Do not bring her into your vile ravings. As for you and this hospital, I will see you gone if it's the last thing I do."

"It just may be the last thing you do here, Dr. Goddard. I would tread carefully if I were you as I don't take well to threats."

Dr. Goddard turned on his heels and stormed out of the room, letting the door slam closed. Nydia released a deep sigh of relief and wiped her trembling, sweaty hands on her lab coat. "I love the perks of my job." Nydia abandoned her attempt for coffee and started back to the ER. She walked straight into Trudy as she opened the door to the lounge.

"Whoa. Slow down. What's the rush?"

"Nothing, my day just sucks." Nydia sighed. "It seems they are sucking more often than not lately."

"Why? What happened?"

"More drama with Dr. Goddard, which makes me rethink whether it's all worth it. Not only do I have to deal with him and the politics of being the head of ER, but also it seems like every time I talk to an abuse victim lately, they go back to their abusers. There is only so much I can take. Maybe I need a break. I could always get a job as a bus driver."

"Oh, come on. Don't let a few bad days bother you. You live on the ER rush, and for every ten victims that go back, there are those one or two who don't. You have a real impact on them."

"I guess, but recently it doesn't feel the way it used to."

"I think you just need some time off with a certain tall detective. I'm sure that would cure most of your ills." Trudy grinned.

Nydia's face lit up. "I'm sure it wouldn't hurt, but I'm not so positive it will cure it though. Nowadays I feel so lost when I'm here. It's so hard to feel like I'm making a difference."

"Look, we're pretty well under control here for now. Why don't you take a break outside for a bit? You know if we need you, I'll call." Trudy put a hand on Nydia's shoulder and gave it a reassuring squeeze.

Nydia thought about it for a moment. "You're right. Maybe I should."

"No maybe about it. Go and call your girl while you're out there."

"My girl. I like the sound of that." Nydia's smile got broader.

"Well, then go call her."

"Thanks, Trudy. I will." Nydia pulled out her cell phone and called Jo's number as she walked away.

Chapter Eleven

THAT EVENING, JO WAS eager to start their first date in what seemed like months but was only a few days. She was excited as she waited outside the restaurant for Nydia. She turned around when she heard a car pull into the gravel driveway and was rewarded with a vision that stopped her heart for a beat and took her breath away.

"Damn."

Nydia walked toward her. She had on a jacket to ward off the fall cold but had it unbuttoned. Jo could see she wore a scoop neck, silk blouse with a pair of dress slacks. The blouse gave a little more than a mere hint of cleavage. *Definitely not workwear.*

Jo brushed off the front of her shirt for any imagined lint, and checked the crease in her own pants. By the time Nydia stood next to her, Jo had her breathing under control again. She looked around before placing a light kiss on Nydia's cheek.

"I hope I haven't kept you waiting," Nydia said.

"Any wait was certainly worth it. You look beautiful tonight."

Nydia blushed and looked down.

Jo thought her demeanor was adorable, but it made her think. *When was the last time someone told her how beautiful she is?* Jo held out her hand. "Shall we go inside, lovely lady?"

Nydia smiled. "I've been looking forward to this ever since I called you and not for the company alone. I'm starving. We were so busy today I never got lunch."

"Well, let's take care of that. I can't have you wither away on me now that we've found time to be together. I think you'll enjoy the food here."

"You've been here before?"

"Yeah, I've been here with my family several times. It's great."

The sparkle in Nydia's eyes vanished.

Jo held the door open for her. "Are you okay, honey? What suddenly made you look so sad?"

"Nothing. I was only thinking."

Before Jo could ask about it more, the hostess approached them and, after confirming Jo's reservation, showed them to their table. She sat them by the window overlooking the vineyard. The sun was setting, coloring the sky a magnificent pink and purple over the green background of the farm.

"Such a magnificent view here. It's almost as lovely as you," Jo said.

As soon as they were settled, Jo put her hand over Nydia's as it rested on the table. Before she had a chance to say anything Nydia spoke.

"I like that you are so close to your mother and sister."

"We are. I've told you my mother and sister mean the world to me. They come first in my life, even above my job."

"Wow. That says a great deal since I know how much your work means to you."

"Yeah, I love my job, especially now working on the IPV Unit."

"Ugh. I wish I felt that way about mine. Lately, it seems like more trouble than fulfillment. It's as if I spend more time dealing with paperwork and politics than my patients," Nydia said, as she looked at the menu. "Then it seems like more than eighty-percent of the people I treat for domestic violence go back to their attackers. Recently, I don't see much point to it. It seems to get harder every day."

"You're right, many do go back. But there are the ones that don't that you have to consider. Those are the ones I do the job for. Being able to get someone out of that kind of violent, hate-filled environment is priceless to me. Now that I'm with the IPV Unit, I get to focus on those."

"I'm just not so sure I agree with it all anymore. Okay, change of subject. We're supposed to be having a good time tonight, not being maudlin."

Before Jo had a chance to get started, the waiter came over to take their orders. When they finished, Jo reached across the table and took Nydia's hand. "I don't know what you have been through, Nydia, but I'm here to listen whenever you want to share."

A slight wistful tone came into Nydia's voice and a hint of sadness. Nydia bent her head and withdrew her hand. "I know. I'm just not ready. I'm sorry, Jo. I know I keep saying that—"

"Nothing to be sorry about. You'll share when you're ready to."

"Thank you for understanding."

"Always."

"You and your sister look a great deal alike. I bet your mother is almost as beautiful."

"Ellie and I get that a lot. Luckily, we both take after my mother. She is beautiful in looks and soul."

"Why do you say luckily?"

"Dad was such a shit, pardon my language, that I don't know what Mom would have done if either of us looked like him. I'm sure it would have been hard on her after all she went through."

"How old were you when they split up?"

"Twelve. Ellie was only seven. Old enough to know what was going on. Now, I do what I do so I can help in the same way my mom was helped. I remember the female police officer who came to the house that last night. She was so nice to us and she made us feel safe until we got to the shelter."

"That's great you had someone watching over you."

"Yeah, it was. I always remember her. She's retired now. Her name is Rose Cutler. I stop by her house to see her and say 'Hello' every once in a while."

"That is so true to the woman you are. Disney couldn't have made a more perfect prince."

"You're crazy, but I think I'll keep you anyway."

"'Keep' me. How generous of you." Nydia sat back in her seat. "Maybe I should rethink this whole thing."

"Please, tell me you're kidding," Jo said in a soft voice that sounded as if she were begging, but she didn't care.

"Oh, honey, of course I'm just kidding."

Jo let out a breath she didn't realize she was holding. "I can't wait for you to meet my family when you're ready to. They'll love you."

Nydia didn't make eye contact. Believing it was nerves on Nydia's part, Jo reassured her. "You'll be fine. Don't worry. They aren't that scary."

"No, it's not that at all."

"Then what is it?"

At that moment, the waiter arrived, and Nydia changed the subject to admiring the food. Jo decided to let the topic of family go. *She'll tell me when she's ready, and on that day, I will be here for her.*

The rest of the evening was perfect. The food, the company, and the conversation were all wonderful. As Always, she found Nydia easy to talk with. Nydia's sense of humor was refreshing with its mix of dry wit and unique view of things.

At the end of the evening, Nydia invited Jo home for coffee, so Jo followed her to the house. Now the two stood outside Nydia's door. She tried to calm her sudden bout of nervousness. She rubbed the palms of her hands on her pants for a second to try to calm her nerves. *You would think I've never been here before.*

Nydia took one of Jo's hands in hers and looked into her eyes. Nydia's hands trembled. *Maybe she's as anxious as I am.* Nydia cleared her throat. "Would you like decaf or regular?"

"Are you sure it's no trouble?"

"Yes. Please?" Nydia asked with a tenderness in her shy smile.

"How could I deny you anything when you look at me that way? Decaf is fine." Jo smiled.

Nydia's smile grew. She opened the door and turned on the lights. "Sit and relax on the couch. I'll be back in a few."

"Okay."

Jo picked up a magazine off the table. She glanced through a few pages until Nydia returned with two mugs. She set the magazine down and took one of the mugs. "Thanks."

"You're welcome." Nydia sat down close enough to her that their thighs touched along their length. Jo's heartbeat quickened and her breathing hitched. It happened whenever she was close to her. Nydia placed her free hand high up on Jo's leg. "I had a wonderful time tonight."

"So did I." Jo's mouth went dry. *Maybe tonight she will let me in.* Before she had a chance to overthink it, Jo leaned in and placed a gentle kiss on Nydia's lips. As she began to pull away, Nydia pulled her closer. Jo placed another kiss but this one grew deeper.

Jo reveled in the play of their lips together. Nydia's were as soft and smooth as velvet. Jo ran the tip of her tongue along Nydia's bottom lip and was rewarded with a moan and an invitation as Nydia's lips parted. Soon their tongues began the sensual dance, and Jo felt a heat and dampness begin to build in her jeans.

They broke apart, taking in ragged breaths. Jo looked into Nydia's eyes and gently caressed her cheeks with the pads of her thumbs. Sure, they had kissed before tonight, but for some reason, these kisses felt so much more intense and impassioned.

"What you do to me with just one kiss is beyond words," Jo said.

"I could say the same. I've never felt this way before with the sparse number of women I've dated over the years. So emotionally out of control, so carefree."

Jo smiled. "Really?"

"Yes, really."

"I want more." Jo moved in for whatever Nydia was willing to offer. The second kiss was more passionate than the first. She was confident in her feelings for Nydia. She knew this was more than anything she had ever experienced before. *I'm in love with you Nydia.* Jo thought. She was afraid saying it out loud would frighten Nydia.

Jo slid one hand deeper into the neckline of Nydia's blouse and caressed the smooth skin of her shoulders. The sounds she heard from Nydia encouraged her. Her other hand slid down Nydia's arm, coming to rest on the swell of her breast and was surprised to realize Nydia wasn't wearing a bra.

Nydia broke off the kiss. "God, your touch feels amazing." She placed searing kisses along Jo's neck.

"I want you so bad, Nydia. Please."

Nydia took a deep breath, pulled away, and shook her head. "I want you just as bad, but we can't."

"Why not? You must sense it too. We were meant for each other. What do you need from me? We've been on this precipice for so long now."

Nydia pulled back more and looked at her. Jo knew Nydia must see the confusion in her eyes. "We can't, I...I don't know how to explain it. This whole thing is so new to me. The feelings I have for you I've never had before with anyone, and they frighten me"

Jo was hurt, not by what Nydia said, but at the realization that Nydia still didn't recognize what they had, and the idea Nydia might not feel the same deep love that she did. Jo regained control over her body and emotions. *How can she not see this as destiny?*

Jo took a deep breath. "It's okay. I'm sorry. I meant what I've said before. We can take this as slow as you want. I'm not going anywhere. I'll wait as long as you need me to." Jo gently touched Nydia's cheek.

Nydia's voice trembled. "Thank you for understanding."

Jo stood up. "I try, and I always will, but I should go now. Thanks for the coffee."

"I'll say you're welcome, even though you never got the chance to drink it. I'm sorry, Jo."

"Again, nothing to be sorry for, okay. I'll talk to you tomorrow. I promise. So, I'll say goodnight for now."

Jo placed a chaste kiss on Nydia's lips

"Then I'll look forward to tomorrow," Nydia said as she touched her own lips.

Jo didn't think Nydia even realized she made the gesture, but Jo found it sensual as hell. "I better go now. Nydia, will you walk me to the car?"

"Sure."

Nydia stopped at the curb while Jo walked around to the driver's side. Jo looked at Nydia and caught her breath. It had grown foggy out and the light from the streetlamp made Nydia look ethereal. With a small wave, Jo got in the car, closed the door, and let out a deep breath. *You undo me, Nydia. I will always give you what you need and want. I just hope someday you realize that.*

Chapter Twelve

NYDIA'S CELLPHONE VIBRATED IN her pocket as she stood at the nurses' station. A smile came across her face when she pulled it out and looked at the caller ID. "Hi, beautiful," she said as she walked away to find some privacy.

"Hi yourself, gorgeous," Jo said.

"Is anything wrong?" Nydia ducked into the doctors' lounge. She clicked the pen in her pocket as she waited for Jo's answer. Nydia was still a bit insecure after their make out session the other night.

"No. I know we didn't have plans, but I was hoping you would agree to dinner at my house tonight. I don't want you to feel pressured, but my mom is sort of insisting. She has the day off and is making a roast with all the fixings. You know she's been dying to meet you, so she asked if I could entice you to come and I promised I'd ask. You can say no if you want. Ellie will be there."

The tension in Nydia's shoulders dissipated only to be replaced by apprehension in her gut. "No. No pressure. Much. No warning and it's only meeting the family." Nydia sighed as she continued to play with the pen.

"Is that a yes or a no?"

Nydia decided to let her heart lead for once. "It's a yes. I would love to meet her too."

"Great. Oh, and she asked Duncan and his wife to join us. My mother hasn't seen them in a while and likes to check up on people."

"Wow, going all out on throwing me into the deep end of the pool, huh?"

Jo laughed. Nydia loved the sound of Jo's laugh, but it did little to relax her now.

"Nydia, I don't want to throw you into anything you don't want to do. If you want to say no, that's fine. I'll understand. Please, honey, don't be afraid." Jo's voice softened as she spoke.

Nydia took a deep calming breath. "I'm just being silly. I would love to meet them. You're right. It will be fine, I'm sure."

"Nothing about your feelings is silly, and it will be fine, I promise."

"You are so good to me. It's no wonder I could so easily fall in love with you." Nydia placed her hand over her mouth, unsure if she had said the last part aloud only to realize she had. Nydia waited for Jo's response, but there was only silence. "I'm sorry—" she started to say.

"Please don't say you're sorry. Only apologize if you didn't mean it," Jo said.

Nydia was at a loss. Her palms grew sweaty and her heart began to beat faster.

"Nydia. I can only tell you I feel closer to you than I have anyone else in my life. I sense we have something very special here. If it's love, then that's what it is. I won't run from that, and I hope you won't either. Please don't."

Nydia felt comforted by Jo's declaration, but she was still hesitant. "I don't know what to do or say, Jo. After the other night, you would think I'd be able to say something at least."

"I don't think you have to. Not for me. Call me a hopeless romantic, but I think we feel what we feel when it's right, and you don't need to label it for me."

"You are a hopeless romantic. But it's a quality I like about you. I'll try to just let it be what it will be for now and not think about it too much. I promise."

"I'm glad to hear that, sweetheart," Jo said.

Nydia wasn't sure if Jo was aware of the endearment, but her soul soaked it up and a smile came to her face. It was the first time she had heard it. Out of the corner of her eye, Nydia saw Trudy heading in her direction at a quick pace. "I have to say goodbye. Trudy is on her way to get me. What time should I be ready tonight?"

"Eight will be fine. That will give you time to get home and change if you want to. I'll pick you up at your place. And please don't stress over it."

"Okay. I won't. I'll see you then."

"Sounds good to me. Now, go back to work and amaze everyone with your awesome skills."

Nydia chuckled. "I will, and the same goes for you. Okay, I really have to say goodbye now. I'll see you tonight."

"Bye, sweetheart," Jo said as she ended the call.

"She called me sweetheart," Nydia said as she hugged the phone to her chest.

"Who did?" Trudy asked with a smile and a devilish look in her eyes. "Anyone I may know?"

"Why, yes. That was Rita in accounting."

Trudy snorted. “Rita in accounting. Yeah. Right. More like one of Riverview’s finest. How is Jo? I haven’t seen her lately.”

“She’s doing just great, thank you very much. She’s been working hard, but we’ve managed to talk on the phone and grab a date here and there when we can.”

“Well, as much as I would love to hear more details, we have a gentleman coming in whose partner beat him up pretty bad. According to the EMTs, he’s a probable head trauma and is unstable. They should be here in five minutes.

“Then let’s get moving.” Nydia left Trudy behind on her race toward the Trauma Room.

***

“Patient was unconscious on scene and hasn’t regained consciousness since,” the EMT said as she and her partner jumped out of the ambulance with the gurney. They followed Nydia into the trauma room. “His BP is 80 by palp. Heart rate is fast and thready at 160. He’s breathing on his own, though respiration is labored. He has multiple contusions to his head and torso. No report of the weapon used. His right eye is swollen, and examination showed fixed and dilated. The other has normal response. We collared him, intubated, started saline IVs, and then ran.”

The team moved the patient to the trauma bed while listening to the EMTs notes.

Nydia began her assessment. The fact he hadn’t regained consciousness worried her. “Were there police there?”

“Yes, but no police were with us or following,” the EMT Nydia knew as Dowd said.

“Why the hell not? Never mind. I don’t have time for that. Wait outside. I want to talk to you two when I’m done.” Nydia began running through the trauma evaluation. She watched as Jordan, one of the respiratory techs, hooked the ventilator to the patient’s tube. Nydia then checked his breathing. His lungs sounded clear of any fluid and his respiration was good. “Okay, Mike, run his blood gases. Trudy, give me the results when he has them. What are his O2 levels, Jordan?”

“O2 is 98%.”

Nydia began looking at the major bruises on his torso and gut. They resembled boot impressions. None of his ribs felt fractured on palpitation. She began looking for more external injuries.

"Doctor, I have the blood gas results. They are within normal limits. However, the results of the CBC indicate a low hematocrit."

"Damn it. It sounds like he is losing blood somewhere. Someone get me the ultrasound."

"I got it," Mike said as he handed her the wand.

Nydia's brows furrowed in concentration as she looked at the monitor. "Looks like his spleen is the cause. Someone call surgery. I want him in the OR stat. Mike, type and crossmatch him. Janet, get the IV fluids pushed as fast as you can."

"Starting to push," Janet said.

"What are his vitals now?" Nydia asked.

Trudy called them out and Nydia was satisfied the patient was stable enough to make the trip. "Okay, people, let's get him upstairs."

Everyone grabbed part of the table and wheeled the patient to the elevator. Once upstairs, Nydia handed her patient off to the surgical team. Now she could focus on her anger, and fumed to herself. *Where are the police, damn it? Someone from IPV should have been here, or at least a uniform.*

***

Nydia walked back to the ER seething. Her jaw was so tight her muscles were getting sore. The EMTs stood up faster than usual when she approached them. "Tell me what happened on scene. Why is there no one from the IPV Unit here? Detective Powers and Reilly, or a detective or officer assigned by them, is supposed to bring in all victims and file reports based on my findings." When neither of the EMTs spoke, Nydia put her hands on her hips and barked, "Well, tell me."

The female EMT, Dowd, shifted on her feet. "When we got on scene, two uniformed officers and a detective were there. I didn't recognize them and didn't get a chance to catch their names. Now that I think about it, I don't think they ever gave them. Did you catch their names, Derek?"

"No, Colleen, I didn't."

"When one of the uniformed officers told the detective that the patient's boyfriend was the assailant, I asked the detective if he wanted to ride along with us to the hospital. The detective said, 'I don't have time for fucking queers and their drama. Let them kill each other for all I care. I got better things to do. Just clean up the mess and get 'em out of here.' I'm sorry for the language Dr. Rogers. I remembered it because the comment was so harsh and cruel. After that, we only had time to scoop and run."

Nydia's anger rose. She glared at Colleen and Derek. The two EMTs looked at each other and took a step back. Nydia realized she was furious at the wrong people. "I'm sorry, guys. It wasn't your fault. Get back to work. I'll handle the police issues and find out what is going on with this." She watched them walk down the hall as she pulled her phone from her pocket. She stepped outside the ER for privacy.

Jo answered on the second ring. "Hey. You missed me already?"

"No, I don't," Nydia said.

"Uhm, okay. Did something come up? Do you need to cancel tonight?"

"I'm calling on an official matter, Detective. As hospital liaison between your unit and the hospital, I demand to know why a victim was brought in here without an officer or detective from your unit accompanying him." She held the phone tight in her grip. "Also, vicious derogatory remarks were made about the victim on scene by a detective. He didn't identify himself, but I assume you can find out and take appropriate actions. I will not stand for it."

Before Jo had a chance to respond, Nydia disconnected the call and shoved the phone into her coat pocket in frustration, anger, and a sense of loss. She took a deep breath to try to calm herself. She ran a trembling hand through her hair and re-entered the ER. Nydia realized she hadn't mentioned dinner.

"I'm too angry right now to think about it. I'll text her when I'm done and cancel." Nydia felt a sense of profound disappointment in Jo and the rest of her team. *I don't know why I'm shocked. I had hoped and prayed Jo was different, but deep down they are all the same.* A few seconds later, her cell phone rang. She looked at the display and saw it was Jo. Nydia turned off the volume and let it go to voicemail.

Chapter Thirteen

JO PUT THE PHONE down for the tenth time in the last hour. She stared at it, let out a sigh, and ran her hand over her face in frustration. Nydia wasn't answering her calls, and she couldn't figure out what happened to make her so angry that she would cancel dinner through a text.

"Shit."

"What's up? I go to lunch and the world collapsed or something?" Duncan asked as he sat down.

"I don't know, at least not yet. Do me a favor, please? Find out about all assaults called in the last six hours or so. I want to know who was involved, victim, suspects, and responding officers. Something is going on, and I want to know what."

"Sure. No problem. I'll call Dispatch," Duncan said.

"Whatever happened must have been major. She sounded so pissed," Jo said to herself. She fidgeted in her chair trying not to think about how cold Nydia's voice had been. She heard Duncan hang up the phone. "So, what did you find out?"

"There were two assaults during the last few hours that required transport to the ER." Duncan looked at his notes. "One was a fight between two teenagers at the high school. One kid who took exception to another kid looking at his girlfriend. It's reported the victim had his jaw broken."

"That doesn't sound like the kind of thing we're looking for. What else do you have?"

"The second may be the one you're interested in then. A twenty-nine-year-old male was transported to Riverview Hospital ER. He was beaten to a pulp and unconscious. Dispatch said an upstairs neighbor reported it. Two guys share the apartment below her and she heard fighting going on. A lot of screaming and crashes, which is why the neighbor became concerned. According to Dispatch, the neighbor stated they were married."

"Do we know who responded to the call? Because I want their damn heads on a platter." Jo picked up her phone and tossed it back on the desk.

"You may be out of luck on that wish. The responding uniform was Junior and his partner."

"Damn it." Jo hit the desk with her fist. "You're right. We're not going to get far there. That moron is out of my reach, unfortunately. We know he's the type to shirk responsibility, but this seems a bit extreme, even for him. Nydia said there was a detective involved. Do we have a name?"

Jo picked up a pen and began clicking it in a quick rhythm. "I feel the need to rip someone apart. If I can get a report out of them, then that might give me some ammunition against Junior."

"Shit out of luck there as well. The detective was Junior's big brother."

"Richard? What the hell was he doing there? He's not on the Unit."

"I don't have a clue, but according to Dispatch he's the one who reported 'on scene'." Duncan circled a section of his notes. "They told me they didn't contact him, so they're not sure how he got the call."

"No, but you and I both know how he got there."

Duncan let his pad fall flat onto the desk. "Junior would be my guess."

"I'd bet my life on it. He must have called him directly."

"Let's track his ass down and find out what's going on." Duncan stood and reached for his coat.

"No need to track him down. It's three o'clock. He'll be at lunch down at Diller's having his usual liquid lunch."

"That guy is a waste of a badge."

Jo adjusted the badge on her belt. "I couldn't agree with you more on that one. Let's go find out what his story is."

"Right behind you."

***

Jo and Duncan entered the pub and paused to let their eyes adjust to the dark interior. After a few seconds, Duncan pointed to a back booth. "There he is."

The two walked to the booth as the waitress placed a new beer in front of Detective Richard Rogers. Based on the number of empties she started piling on her tray, he had been there a while.

As she walked away, Richard looked up at them as Jo and Duncan slid in across from him.

"What the hell do you two want? Can't you see I'm busy?"

"Yeah, I can tell, Dick," Jo said with an insincere grin.

"Fuck off, Powers." Richard put his drink down with enough force to spill some of its contents. "And the name is Richard, bitch."

"I'm not leaving until I get some explanation from you." Jo leaned back and put her arm along the back of the booth, resting it behind Duncan. "What were you doing on a call related to my unit without informing me?"

"What the fuck are you talking about?"

"Don't be stupid, Dick. The call you went on this morning with Junior. You knew it was my unit who should have handled it, so what were you doing there to begin with? You weren't called by Dispatch, or anyone else according to the call logs."

Jo grinned as his face turned red.

"It's none of your fucking business what calls I go on. You're not my supervisor. As for not calling in your guys, there was no reason. It was just a couple of fags beating on each other. What does it matter if they fucking kill each other? Two less perverts the world has to deal with." He sneered at Jo.

Jo's fury rose. She put both arms on the table and leaned forward. Her hands clenched so tight her fingernails dug into her palms. She wanted to knock his teeth in. Duncan put a hand on her arm, reminding her he was there and that they were in public.

Jo took a deep breath and stood up. "You're the one who's scum, Dick. There's only one reason you still have a badge, and we all know it. I'm going forward with this, and you can damn well count on your actions being in my report."

"Fuck you, Powers. If you want to waste your time on a couple of fags, be my guest. As far as your report goes, we all know where that is going to end up, in the garbage where it belongs. You can't touch me and you know it."

Jo ground her teeth together to keep from screaming in Richard's face. She scowled at him with her teeth gritted. "Someday, Dick, you're going to fuck up so bad, no one will be able to protect your ass. Come on, Duncan. Let's get out of here before I have to take a shower to get his dirt off of me."

Duncan followed her out of the pub.

Jo squinted against the sudden assault of light on her eyes. "Let's go to the hospital, find out what we can, and check on the status of the victim," she said as they got in the car.

"Sure thing. I hope they thought to gather and protect any evidence they could. We'll also have to send some uniforms down to secure the scene and check it out."

"Probably too late for that. The scene has likely been trampled over by now and useless to us. But you're right. We should send our people down to take a look." Jo let out a deep sigh. She thought about all the things they now had to do to clean this mess up, and she still had to get Nydia to talk to her so she could explain what happened. "This sucks. Let's get going."

Duncan started the car. "On a weird note, isn't Nydia's last name Rogers?"

"Yeah, but I doubt she's related to that asshole. One of the founding families of Riverview was Rogers. The name is as common around here as Smith. Besides, I'm sure she would have mentioned it."

"Yeah, you're right. I can't see her related to those guys." Duncan put the car in drive and pulled out of the parking lot.

Chapter Fourteen

AS SOON AS JO and Duncan entered the ER, Jo was on the lookout for Nydia. She was so engrossed with looking, she bumped into someone.

"If you come in here, you better have your body armor on. You're in enemy territory right now," Trudy said, a scowl on her face.

Jo swallowed hard. "She's that mad, huh?"

"No, Detective, we're all that mad."

"I can explain, really. I honestly only found out about it when Nydia called. It's a total mess, I know. Is Nydia here? I need to talk to her."

Trudy stared at Jo. "Nydia's in with a patient, but she should be done in a few minutes."

"Thank you so much."

"Don't thank me yet. I don't know that I'm doing you a favor."

Jo sighed and her shoulders slumped. "I know I have to make things right. You know she's important to me, more than anyone."

"You're important to her, too. I think she's more upset because it's your team that's involved. Getting her to understand that what happened was beyond your control, which I assume it was, is going to be the hard part. I don't know what the screw up was, or who did it, but as the person in charge of the unit, she is holding you accountable."

"I know, and I'll try anything to make up for it. She's right though, my unit is my responsibility."

Jo looked over Trudy's shoulder and saw Nydia walk out of one of the exam rooms, looking at the tablet in her hand. Nydia didn't acknowledge her as she laid the tablet on the nurses' station. Then she turned toward Jo. As their eyes met, Jo's heart fluttered as it always did when they were together. Her heart sank when all she saw in Nydia's face was anger. Nydia turned and went toward her office.

"Go on, follow her," Trudy said.

"I appreciate it. Thanks."

"Go before she has a chance to dwell on it more. I'm sure you'll be okay. I know you mean more to her than anyone. Be honest and let her know what happened." Trudy put her hand on Jo's and gave it a quick squeeze, and then let go.

"I couldn't be anything else." Jo knew that her future happiness might be on the line. *I couldn't bear a life without her*, she thought. Her chest tightened as Jo put her hand on the office doorknob, determined to make Nydia understand. She took a deep breath and knocked gently. She opened the door and entered before Nydia had a chance to refuse her. Jo was ready to fight for their happiness.

Nydia stood in front of the small window with her back to the door. She rested her hand on the sill and let out a sigh as her shoulders slumped. "What do you want, Jo?" Nydia asked without turning around. "I've said what I had to say, and I don't think there's much to add now."

She sounded tired. Jo stepped further into the room. "Nydia, don't do this. Please, honey, let me explain. I didn't know there was an issue until you called."

Nydia placed her other hand on the windowsill but didn't turn around.

"No one from my unit was here because we weren't notified." Jo took several steps closer.

Nydia turned to face her. "I don't have time for your excuses, Detective, and that's what it sounds like." Her eyes glistened with unshed tears. "I thought you were different. I believed in you."

That cut Jo deeper than any knife could. She considered her next words as she thought, *I refuse to let us end like this. It can't. I won't let it happen.* She took a step closer. "Please, Nydia, you can believe in me. I never would have let this happen. You know my story. How much these victims mean to me. In this situation, I would have been here myself, or made sure someone from the unit was."

Nydia didn't respond.

Jo stepped closer still. "Please, let me have my say, and then you can tell me to go. But we deserve the chance for me to explain."

Nydia stared at her, and then turned to look out the window again. After a few moments, when she said nothing and made no move to make Jo leave, Jo grasped at the opportunity.

"When you called, that was the first time I was aware something happened. I had Duncan called Dispatch to find out what had gone down. We tracked back the call and found the name of the responding uniform and detective. The officer didn't call in the assault to my unit, or any other unit. He called the one detective he knew wouldn't care. He was right." Jo took another step closer.

"The detective ignored everything he was supposed to do. He

never notified us. Instead, he swept the whole thing under the carpet. I confronted him and he admitted everything," Jo said as tears stung her eyes. She refused to give into them. Crying now wasn't going to help her.

"I never would have let this go, and I won't let it. I'm going to make it right. I'll do my best to make sure these officers are reprimanded."

Nydia turned toward her as Jo finished her plea. Her face was wet with tears. Without a thought, Jo gathered her in her arms.

"Don't cry, baby. Yell at me if you have to, or tell me you don't believe me, but please don't cry. I feel so helpless when you do." Jo's own tears began fall.

"I want to believe you. Really I do."

"You can, Nydia. Just look in your heart. You know I would never lie to you. You mean the world to me."

After a few seconds, Nydia's body relaxed and she let out a quiet sob. They stood holding each other until Nydia's crying began to subside.

Jo pulled back and lifted Nydia's chin, so their eyes met. "Do you believe me?"

"Yes, I believe. I'm sorry I doubted you."

"I will never do anything to make you doubt me or my feelings for you."

"I know you will do your best to hold them responsible, Jo, but I won't be surprised though if nothing comes out of the report."

"I will try my best to make it. So, are we okay now?"

Nydia gave Jo's body a squeeze that reassured her, "Yes, we're fine, more than fine."

"Can I tell my mother that you're still coming tonight?"

"Would you mind if we put it off? I'm emotionally drained right now, and I just want to curl up with you on my couch tonight."

Jo smiled and her heart beat faster at the thought. "I would love nothing more. They can wait. I'll call Mom and tell her to reschedule us."

"Thank you."

Jo kissed Nydia's lips.

Chapter Fifteen

THE NEXT FRIDAY, NYDIA got off work early after working out a deal with another doctor who owed her a favor. Now she stood at the foot of her bed, freshly showered, and dressed in her underwear. Most of the contents of her closet were laying on the bed, and Jo was due any minute to take her to the rescheduled dinner with Jo's family. Nydia's ability to make a simple decision had abandoned her.

Nydia's only comparison to family was her mom and her little brother Stevie. But this was different, more intense. This family was a living, breathing unit, not a memory from the distant past. Nydia glanced at the clock. She was out of time. She took a deep breath and grabbed a pair of beige slacks and the green silk blouse that complimented her eyes. The doorbell rang as she finished the last button. After one last look in the mirror, Nydia went downstairs.

She opened the door to find Jo standing on her doorstep, and Nydia's stomach fluttered. She slowly ran her eyes over Jo. She looked beautiful in her tight jeans and the red chambray shirt that contrasted with her dark hair. Jo held her coat over her arm. Nydia took in the vision and thought, *I hope I never get used to this.*

"What's the matter? My socks don't match?" Jo asked with a grin and a glance at her feet.

Nydia regained her focus and cleared her tight throat. "Uhm, no. It's just you look great. But aren't you a bit chilled?"

"Well, you look beautiful so we're even. Though in truth, I think you're ahead. Nope, the car is warmed up for you. Your chariot awaits." Jo pointed to the car.

Nydia blushed and glanced away.

"Are you ready to go?" Jo asked.

"Yeah, let me just lock up." The sound of the lock seemed loud to her, or was she being super aware because Jo was here? As Nydia turned back, she was caught off balance when Jo took her hand, pulled her close, and kissed her. They broke apart, each taking a deep breath with Nydia's hands on Jo's chest for support.

"I've been dying to do that since we talked on the phone this afternoon. You do something to me, Nydia, that no one else ever has. The mere sound of your voice sets me off with desire." She rested her forehead against Nydia's.

Nydia knew how important this moment was. She couldn't do anything but be honest to Jo, and herself. "I feel the same way, Jo. But I get scared by you, by all this emotion."

"Why?"

"I don't know how to explain it." Nydia laid a hand on Jo's cheek. "It's just that you've come to mean so much to me. You are becoming my whole world. That's what scares me, not you. It's that it feels so fast and so deep. It's like nothing I've ever felt before." Nydia drew Jo's face closer to her own, and this time the kiss was deep and passionate. Their tongues dueled in a battle of want and need.

When they broke apart for lack of air, Jo pulled away a little and looked deep into Nydia's eyes. "I'm sorry about last week," Jo murmured.

"You already apologized several times. I've told you, you have nothing to be sorry about. If anyone should say how sorry they are, it should be me."

"I messed up and it caused you to doubt me."

"I should be the one with regret, Jo, not you. I should've known better and believed in you. You've shown me enough to recognize that you're more than the average police officer. You care about these cases. You've told me that, but I let my anger cloud my heart. I'm sorry I ever doubted you."

"There's nothing to be sorry for, honey. Though I hope someday you feel comfortable enough to share why you have such issues with the police. When you do, I believe we can move past it together."

"I will. Only I'm not there quite yet. Soon, I promise to try for soon."

"Okay, I'll be here when you're ready. Let's get going. I can't wait for you to meet everyone," Jo said with a broad smile.

"All right, let's do this."

Chapter Sixteen

WHEN JO PARKED IN the driveway, Nydia let out a deep sigh. She gave Nydia's arm a gentle, reassuring squeeze. "There's nothing to worry about. I promise. They'll love you."

"It's all right. I'm just a little nervous."

"Well, don't be. It'll be fine."

Nydia took a deep breath and let it out slowly. "Okay. Let's do this," she said as she climbed out of the car.

Jo looked at her over the roof of the car. "Babe, it's not a firing squad. Honest."

Nydia let out a nervous laugh. "I know. I'm just over-reacting."

"Come on. I'll be right beside you."

Together they walked up to the door. As Jo let them in, raucous laughter came from the back of the house. She wasn't surprised. Her mother's kitchen was always the center of any event they had. She made it warm and inviting to anyone who entered.

With a gentle touch on Nydia's back, Jo guided her toward the kitchen. When they came in, everyone turned toward them. Nydia's muscles tightened.

"There is nothing to worry about, remember I'm here for you, always," Jo whispered in her ear.

"I know." Nydia smiled.

Jo let go. "Hi everybody. What are we missing?"

"Nothing but your mother sharing some of your more adventurous childhood tales," Duncan's wife, Maddy, answered with a small laugh.

"Oh God, shoot me now."

"Why? Your embarrassment is my favorite part of these get-togethers," Duncan said.

"See if you get coffee in the morning from me," Jo said. "Let me take this opportunity to introduce you all to Nydia. Nydia, you know Duncan of course. This lovely woman with the smirk on her face is his wife, Maddy."

"Nice to meet you," Nydia said.

Maddy pulled Nydia into a heartfelt hug. "It's our pleasure to finally meet the woman who has become so important to Jo. Duncan can't stop raving about you and your work at the hospital."

"I see you left the munchkin home," Jo said.

"Yes. Even though the little rugrat was loathe to let us go. Every time I walked away, he cried. Poor thing," Maddy said.

"You should've brought him. You know I love seeing him."

"I know, but today was grownup day. They happen so rarely."

"Okay. But promise for next time."

"I swear," Maddy said.

Jo continued with the introductions. "This radiant woman is my sister Electra." Jo grinned at her sister's frown. "Just don't call her that, if you value your life."

"Hi, Nydia. I know we've seen each other around the hospital, but it's nice to see you here," Ellie said with a broad smile.

"Hi, Ellie. It's good to see you too," Nydia said.

"And last, but far from least, is my mother, Cassandra. The only person who can still kick my ass."

"Language." Cassandra swatted Jo on said body part. "Welcome to our home, Nydia." She pulled Nydia in for a long and firm hug.

"Thank you. Thank you for having me," Nydia said when she was let go.

Jo noticed Nydia's voice crack a little. "So, which story are we covering at the moment?"

"The one about you, Mr. Wesley, and the case of indecent exposure."

"I've said it multiple times, it was an accident. Besides, it wasn't my fault that he was walking past with his dog at that particular moment."

Ellie let out a snort. "I think poor Brutus was emotionally scarred for life. As I recall, he never came near you after that."

"Brutus was a coward," Jo said with a laugh.

"Brutus was a sixty-five-pound Boxer, dear," Cassandra said.

"He was still a baby about the whole thing." Jo pouted.

Jo heard Nydia chuckle next to her and it was music to her soul. She bumped her in the shoulder. "No comments from you either." Jo grinned.

"Wouldn't dream of it, Lady Godiva," Nydia said. Everyone, including Nydia, laughed.

Jo glared at her, but her look softened into a smile when Nydia poked her tongue out at her. "You're impossible, you know that, but I love you anyway."

Nydia's eyes grew wide. "Uhm, did you just say you loved me?"

Jo shifted from one foot to another, and her eyes darted back and forth. Everyone filed out of the room, leaving Jo and Nydia alone.

"I'm sorry, Nydia. I didn't mean to say that," she said, worried she had been too forthcoming.

"Do you mean you don't love me?" Tears welled up in Nydia's eyes.

Jo's heart beat faster and her hands became clammy.

After a few moments of silence, Nydia turned away and wiped the back of her hand over her eyes. Jo heard her sniffle.

"Nydia, please don't cry." Jo reached out to touch Nydia's shoulder.

"I'm sorry, Jo. I didn't mean to make this harder for you." Nydia turned back to face Jo, her eyes glistening. "I should just go. Please tell everyone I said goodbye. I'll show myself out."

"Nydia, it's not what you think. I promise."

"I think it's been made pretty obvious now."

Jo heard the hurt tone in her voice.

"There's no need for you to say anything more. I'll call a cab outside," Nydia said with a shuddering sigh. "But know that even if you don't love me, I was starting to fall in love with you. Goodbye, Jo."

Jo was stunned. "She loves me," Jo said to herself as Nydia walked away with Cassandra following behind.

"Oh, shit!" Jo said as it hit her that Nydia had left the room.

"Go on you idiot, follow her, Ellie said

Jo burst through the kitchen doorway and ran down the hall. She came to a stop when she caught sight of Cassandra and Nydia in a hug. Cassandra whispered in Nydia's ear and let go, stepping out of the hallway. Nydia opened the front door.

"Wait. I do have something to say. If you still want to go when I'm done, fine, but I hope you'll stay."

Nydia stood with her hand on the doorknob.

"I love you." Jo put her hand over Nydia's. "I truly and deeply do. I'm sorry I froze back there. I was scared, scared that I had frightened you off. I thought it was too much to say it and that you would feel pressured in some way. I'm sorry, Nydia. I never meant to hurt you. I don't know what I would do if you left now."

Nydia looked at their hands. "You really love me?"

Jo smiled and moved so they were facing each other. "Yes. I do." She wiped away a tear as it began to slide down Nydia's face. She leaned in and laid a gentle kiss on Nydia's lips. "I'm sorry my silence hurt you."

"It's just that no one has ever said that to me before," Nydia said.

"Well, I do. I do love you." Jo kissed her again.

Nydia returned the kiss.

That Nydia loved her was all Jo could think of. Nydia pulled away from her and Jo watched as her mother took Nydia in her arms in a warm embrace.

"Welcome to the family. Now I have a nurse, and a doctor as daughters," Cassandra said, holding her at arm's length but not letting go.

Jo and Nydia's eyes met, and they both smiled.

Chapter Seventeen

AS NYDIA EXITED THE ER, her breath caught when she saw Jo leaning against her car. It had been a few days since the dinner at Jo's house. Now, whenever she had a spare moment, Jo was almost all she could think about. Here it was the following Tuesday, and she was looking forward to them spending the evening together. Maybe she could find the words to let Jo know how deeply in love she was with her. Gone were any residual doubts. This was love, and she knew it with every fiber of her being.

Jo stood up as Nydia stopped in front of her. "So, how was the day in the trenches?" Jo rested her hands on Nydia's hips.

The warmth of Jo's fingers seeped through Nydia's shirt. The action seemed so natural. Nydia had no reference but imagined this was what coming home felt like. "Not too bad. No traumas came in today. It was just your average day-to-day emergencies. How was yours?"

"There is nothing average about anything you ever do." Jo placed a quick kiss on Nydia's lips. "My day was busy. We had a lot of follow up and paperwork to do the last few days with Barbara's case and several others. We thought we had a new lead, but I still haven't been able to track down her husband. I only wish I could figure out where he's holed up."

Jo ran her fingers through her hair. It was a gesture Nydia had come to find familiar and endearing, but she missed being held. Nydia took Jo's other hand in hers. "Don't beat yourself up, honey. I know you and Duncan are doing everything you can."

Jo smiled and let out a deep sigh. "You're right. We'll need another statement from Barbara now that she has had more time to think about what happened. See if she knows anything about the new lead. We'll also ask her about any other friends or relatives she thinks may be willing to hide him. We've checked the ones we think would. But for now, we're still looking. He must be getting help from somewhere and someone, and I'll be damned if I can figure out who."

"How about the other case? The one you didn't know about?

Richard Neilson? The gay man?"

"We arrested the husband. How is Richard by the way? Will he be okay?"

"He's been moved to the rehab unit in the hospital, but the surgery to remove his spleen went well. It's just a matter of getting him mobile again. I guess as the lead detective I can tell you this much, he lost a great deal of memory and motor function as a result of the brain trauma. It's so sad. He was a graduate student and now he's lost that."

Jo stepped closer so they were almost standing as one. "It's been a long week. We hardly talked, and I love you. That's all I want to concentrate on tonight." She reached out and, with a gentle touch, pushed an errant bit of hair behind Nydia's ear. "I can't seem to keep from touching you. I hope you're okay with it, because I think it's become a habit of mine."

Nydia reveled in the warmth and love Jo gave her. For the first time in many years, someone cared for her with deep and genuine tenderness. Nydia still had some doubts in the back of her mind, but they were becoming fewer and fewer. It was the only time since she was a small child that she could remember being happy. Yet she was afraid of being overwhelmed.

"I'm more than fine with it," Nydia said. Jo stepped back and opened the door for Nydia to get in.

As she waited for Jo to come around the car and join her, Nydia tried to examine her thoughts for a moment. It was as if she was waiting for a shoe to drop on her happiness. Nydia jumped in her seat when she felt Jo's smooth palm on her cheek pulling her back to the world around her. Nydia was so lost she hadn't noticed Jo sit down. With a slowness Nydia could barely stand, Jo placed a light kiss on her lips.

"Don't go from me. It hurts when you do," Jo said in a quiet voice, while her thumb caressed Nydia's cheek.

Nydia sighed. "I'm sorry. Sometimes I feel a little dazed by you. Well, not you in particular. Rather, because of how much we feel for each other. It seems like I've known you forever. But my brain knows that isn't true. Does that make any sense? I'm sorry for sounding so confused."

"Yeah, it does, but in a good way I think." Jo put her lips to Nydia's forehead before pulling away.

Nydia smiled as the love Jo had for her engulfed her soul.

Jo looked at her a moment longer. "I'm willing to spend an eternity convincing you. For now, how about we spend a quiet evening having dinner out?"

"I can do that." Nydia smiled.

"Well, then let's get going. We're losing precious daylight here, woman." Jo's broad smile was infectious.

"Geez, pushy much?" Nydia chuckled.

Jo laughed. "Only when I need to be, love. Only when I need to be."

The endearment surprised Nydia because it still seemed so surreal to her that, despite what she put her through, Jo Powers loved her.

Once settled in the car, Nydia rested her hand on Jo's over the gearshift knob. They spent the ride chatting about their day. Jo talked about her mother and sister. Nydia missed the idea of family, and if she wanted to join Jo's, she needed to lay to rest all her internal conflict about the police and family. Over twenty years of anger and hatred were enough. It was time for her to move on with her life. Jo was a good cop, a wonderful woman, and someone who loved her. Nydia would learn to change. She wanted to and it was time.

Chapter Eighteen

JO PARKED HER CAR by the riverfront a few blocks from the restaurant. "I thought you'd enjoy a stroll on the boardwalk before we eat," Jo said as she stepped out. She leaned back in. "I know it's chilly, but I promise to keep you warm."

Nydia smiled as Jo came around to her side and opened the door. She felt the cool wind and shivered a little. "That's a sweet thought. I like that," she said as Jo wrapped an arm around her shoulders. "I think it's a great idea. It's a nice evening for it after being holed up in the ER all week." Nydia looked at the moon over the water as they began walking. The reflection on the river and the moon above were picture perfect. "It's so spectacular I wish I had my camera with me. I usually keep my small one in the car for just such occasions."

"Why didn't I know you did photography. Hmm. We'll have to get you a second one to keep in my car."

Nydia felt she could gaze forever into Jo's warm, blue eyes. They sparkled in the moonlight.

Jo and Nydia began their stroll to the restaurant. Jo gave her shoulder a gentle squeeze as they walked. Nydia glanced over at the hand wrapped around her and realized how right it felt. It had been so long since she had felt the comfort and affection she did when with Jo. *Maybe the idea of home isn't so impossible if it's with Jo. To have the sense of family that she has with hers would be wonderful*, she thought.

When she heard the sound of heavy footsteps behind them, Nydia tried to pull away from Jo, but Jo offered a comforting smile, and pulled her in closer. Nydia let her and felt safe.

"Hey, Powers. Is this your new piece of ass?" a voice Nydia recognized from her past said.

Nydia stopped and ripped away from Jo's grip. She didn't turn around. She refused to. She looked down so her hair could shield her.

The speaker drew closer. "I didn't think cute blondes were your type. I always thought of you as a little more for the slut look. Going by the clothes, this one almost looks innocent—definitely not your style."

Jo spun around. "Junior, shut the fuck up. You've already crossed the line as far as I'm concerned. Don't push me further. You won't like it."

Nydia began to tremble as the anger around her grew. She felt as if years had never passed and she was being assaulted by the same anger, and taunting from her youth.

Junior took another step forward. "So, who's the one you got your perverted hooks into this time?" Before there was a chance to react, Junior grabbed Nydia by the arm and spun her around. She came face to face with her attacker, one she recognized too well.

"Well, well. I guess you do go for the sluts. Hi, Nydia. Long time no see." Junior stared at Nydia with a glint of hatred and contempt.

Nydia stood paralyzed by fear, both old and new. Of course, she had seen Junior over the last several years. It was a small town and their jobs guaranteed the occasional run-in. However, he had never looked at her with so much venom and antagonism before.

Jo stared at them. "You know each other?"

Junior sneered at Nydia before giving Jo a smug grin. "Sure, you mean she didn't tell you? This is too good." Junior laughed. "Go ahead and tell her, sis. It's obvious you haven't."

Nydia's uncharacteristic silence continued.

Junior laughed louder this time.

"Sister?" Jo exclaimed as she looked at Nydia. "He's your brother?"

Nydia glanced over and knew Jo was putting the pieces of the puzzle together. She looked Jo in the eyes. "Yes."

Jo looked back and forth between the brother and sister. Nydia was hurt by the expression on her face, but she felt helpless.

Nydia's brother, Steven Rogers, Jr., rocked on his heels, his eyes wide with satisfaction, and his smile broad and cocky.

Nydia was sure Jo could see the resemblance, now that the two were face to face. Nydia had put this part of her life in the dark corners of her mind. Now though, the look of confusion and hurt on Jo's face ripped at her heart.

"So, I guess this means you're still a fucking dyke," Junior said to Nydia. His disgust oozed from his body. "If mom were still alive, she would be so proud."

Nydia stared at him hard. Her anger grew too large to keep locked inside. That plus Jo being by her side, gave her the courage she needed.

"Don't bring her into this, Stevie. You were barely five when she died. You don't know what she would want. You don't know anything about her. So, you sure as hell don't have the right to say anything about her. But I do. I know she would only want me to be happy. Before she died, she told me not to end up like her. To get away from them. So, don't even think of starting that crap."

"Well, at least Dad doesn't have to put up with your shit anymore. You've been a selfish bitch your whole life and the biggest disappointment in his life. You left us to survive on our own. Why? So you could go off to fucking college and be a rug muncher. You're the one who chose to leave, not us." Junior's anger seethed from him. "He always said you were a useless perversion and slut, not worth enough to care about. It was true back then and even truer now. I don't know why I'm bothering to waste my breath on you, other than the enjoyment I'm getting from the look on your girlfriend's face right now. Go have fun with her and put that mouth of yours to use for once. Powers could use a good fuck."

Jo shoved him, making him take several steps back. "Shut your asinine, stupid, Neanderthal brain off, Junior. You might hurt yourself with it." She put herself between him and Nydia, her hands clenched and shaking at her sides. Her entire body seemed to hum.

"What's that supposed to mean?" He pushed Jo back to force her off balance but failed since she was taller, and had a great deal more muscle.

Contempt crossed Jo's face. "Figure it out with that miniscule thing you call a brain, you moron."

Nydia was afraid of what Jo might do to him. She put her hand on the small of Jo's back.

Jo glanced towards her and attempted a reassuring smile. Nydia could still feel Jo's tense muscles.

Junior found his nerve again. "Fuck off, Powers. You're just pissed because you know messing with the likes of her will ruin your career. Stick with her and you might as well kiss your career goodbye. Have fun with your new plaything, Powers. She's going to cost you dearly."

He tipped his hat back and placed his hand on the handle of his Taser.

"Dykes!" he said, bumping Jo's shoulder as he passed.

Before he was out of view, he turned back and made a gesture, putting his finger to the corner of his eye. Nydia recognized the childhood warning. It signaled her father was on the warpath.

Chapter Nineteen

NYDIA STOOD FROZEN IN place, tears running down her face. She wiped at them with her sleeve and wished she could run home.

"Are you okay?" Jo asked in a hard but concerned voice.

"Yeah. Just give me a minute. I'll be fine." Nydia turned her back on Jo to hide her hurt and humiliation.

Jo sighed. Nydia couldn't tell if it was out of frustration or disappointment.

She placed a hand on Nydia's back and rubbed it. "No, you're not, you're shaking. Come on. There's a diner right down the alleyway. You look like you could use a strong cup of tea or coffee."

Nydia's desire to run and hide grew. It was what she had done all her life. Jo moved her arm around Nydia's shoulder again and guided her down the sidewalk.

Nothing has changed, damn it. It's as if I'm sixteen again. Nydia's shoulders slumped as old emotions overwhelmed her. *Why am I even considering being with Jo? My family has broken me. They'll win now...they always have and always will.*

She hadn't been paying attention to where they were going until Jo opened the door of the diner for her. Nydia was grateful when Jo led her to a booth in the back, and away from the few patrons sitting at the front counter. She didn't want to have to face anyone right now. Instead, she stared at the tabletop. A few minutes after they sat, a waitress placed a cup of hot cocoa in front of her.

Nydia looked at her confused. "I didn't order this."

"I figured you needed it," Jo said from across the table. There was an unusual tightness in Jo's voice. Nydia knew it was on her to make this better. She just didn't know how.

"Thank you," she said, avoiding eye contact. "I'm sorry for what happened back there. You shouldn't have had to find out like this."

Jo let out a sigh. "Did you ever intend on telling me?" She ran her fingers through her hair and then let her hand drop to the table.

Nydia sat silent for a moment and then opened her mouth to

speak.

Jo stopped her by going first. "Nydia, I believe you have a reason for not telling me about your family. But right now, I'm hurt, and I'll admit, a bit angry." Jo took a sip of her coffee, holding the cup tight. With a deep breath, she put the cup on the table and her hands around it. "Damn it, Nydia. I don't understand, and I want to. I truly do. But why wouldn't you share something so important with me? This isn't just about me and my feelings. It's also about my career." Jo's eyes were moist.

Nydia got up the courage to try and explain. "I know it's hard to understand—"

"No, let me finish, Nydia, because I don't think you can know how I feel. To be honest, I mostly feel betrayed. After all the miscommunications we've had about my job, you chose not to tell me about your family. You had to know it was going to affect me professionally, and us personally, and yet you consciously decided not to share. I know you're hurt by what just happened, but you have to understand, so am I." Jo took another deep breath and let it out slowly.

After a moment of silence between them, she reached across the table and took hold of Nydia's trembling hands. The warmth from her touch seeped through to Nydia's soul.

"When your brother confronts us, and you're silent, it tells me how you see me and us, and even yourself. It feels like you don't care about any of that, at least not enough to stand up for them. I thought we meant more to each other. If I'm wrong, tell me now." Jo let go of her.

Nydia looked up with a start. "No, God no, you're not wrong. I can't get over how much you mean to me. You've come to be my world. With you by my side, I can fight this...them. I think that was the first time I've ever stood up for myself against any of them. Maybe with you in my life, I can become whole again once and for all. No more doubt, no more uncertainty about myself and us, or you. I've never felt like this before. When I'm around you, it's as if anything is possible. I love you, Jo." Nydia looked down, hiding her eyes. "I guess I thought that feeling was enough to block out the rest of the world and fix things."

"Well, it didn't, Nydia." Jo ran her fingers through her hair again and then took hold of Nydia's hand once more. "The part that is really making me upset is you didn't tell me that your family treats you so callously, and with such anger and hatred. I would have understood so much more about you if only you'd told me. I can only imagine that your growing up with that kind of emotional abuse would instill mistrust in anyone, especially when they are police officers." Jo ran her fingers gently along the back of Nydia's hand. "But it wasn't fair to me, not without telling me why."

Nydia nearly cried at the hurt tone in Jo's voice. "I'm sorry, Jo, I was so wrong not to have told you. I also know I should have said something to him this time." She wasn't able to call him by name, or even brother. "But once I realized it was him, I froze. I turned back into that little kid everyone in that house hated. Every day I had to put up with that kind of stuff, from him, my older brother, and even from my dad. My dad was the worst. When Mom died, he was the one person left in my life who was supposed to love me unconditionally."

Nydia grabbed a napkin and wiped her eyes. "My mother tried to protect me from most of it, but she was as much of a target as I was. She died when I was nine, and then there was no one. Not even my little brother. Right after she died, he was the only one I cared about. I wanted so much to protect him from them. But in the end, they got him to turn against me too.

Jo lifted their hands and kissed Nydia's palm. "I shot off before understanding where you were coming from," Jo said as she lowered their hands.

Nydia reveled in the gentleness of the gesture. "You had no way of knowing and every reason to react. I don't blame you for being angry. You're right...I should have told you sooner."

"I would have thought you were comfortable enough with us, to share with me sooner." Jo took a sip of coffee.

"When my mom died it was so scary and confusing. That night she and my dad had been fighting. That was normal for him. It was loud, so loud I hid in little Stevie's room. I hid him in the closet, as I always did, trying to keep him calm. I heard shouting and then mom screaming. There was the sound of things breaking. All at once, it seemed, there was the ambulance, and all these police officers and detectives in the house. But no one seemed to be doing anything. When it was all over, Mom was gone. I saw her taken out on a gurney, and then Richard told me she was dead. From then on, I thought my father somehow had the power of life and death, because she left, and he didn't." Nydia looked into Jo's eyes, seeking strength from her.

"My older brother, Richard, always told me I was just like her. That someday my mouth would get me in trouble like hers had. After mom died, they expected I would take her place and fill the void left in the house. My childhood ended that day." Nydia looked up at Jo, tears streaming down her face.

"At first, I was so angry at her for that. I felt like I could never love her again. Over the years I let them convince me I wasn't worth loving, that I was useless to everyone. It took a lot for me to believe in myself. Let alone enough to think I could be a doctor someday. Finally, I got away from them. I went to college and made something of myself. It was the hardest thing I had ever done." She finished with a sob.

Jo jumped up and went and sat beside her. She held her in a soothing embrace while she cried. Nydia buried her face in Jo's chest as Jo whispered in her ear. "I believe, wherever your mother's spirit may be, she looks down on you with love. I'm also sure she realizes you love her. Moms always know that. And I love you too, with my whole heart."

Nydia pulled back enough to look up at Jo and saw the depth of Jo's convictions staring back at her. "Can I hold onto you for a few moments?"

"You can hold on to me forever."

"I think I will."

"I'm counting on it. I love you, Nydia. Always know that, even when I'm angry and frustrated."

"I love you too," Nydia admitted fully and with all her heart.

Jo stood up and placed some money on the table. "Come on. Let's go home." She stretched out her hand for Nydia to take.

Chapter Twenty

THEY LEFT THE DINER and made their way back to the car without any further drama, for which Jo was grateful. *Right now, I'm too exhausted for anything.* She lost the fight to stifle a yawn.

Ten minutes later, Jo stopped the car in Nydia's driveway. She looked across at Nydia sleeping in the passenger seat. Her eyes were closed and a little puffy from crying, and her hair was mussed from sleeping against the window, but she was still the most beautiful woman Jo knew.

Nydia woke up and looked out the window. "Oh. Did I doze off? I'm sorry, Jo. I'm not a very good date tonight."

Her smile was tired and weak, and her eyes had lost their shine, but Jo's heart still skipped a beat. "Only for a few minutes, and you are always my idea of a perfect date, even if you only want to sit inside all day and watch out the window as the grass grows."

"So, we're here already."

"Yup, door to door service," Jo said with a smile.

"And very good service it was too. Thank you."

"No problem, ma'am. Our pleasure, but please remember to tip the driver."

Nydia leaned in and kissed Jo long and deep enough for Jo to feel as if it was the first time again.

"Is that sufficient?"

Once her head cleared, Jo smirked. "I'm not sure that will cover the full twenty percent."

Nydia leaned in again. This time the kiss deepened as soon as their lips met. Jo reached up behind Nydia's neck. Their tongues were darting at each other, but then moved to sensual strokes along the sides, and then round and round. Jo relished the silky feel and the taste of Nydia's mouth. She didn't think she could ever get her fill of it. Jo had to break it off to draw in much-needed oxygen.

"God, I've missed you the last few days."

"I've missed you too." Nydia tried to straighten her collar with trembling fingers.

Jo reached over and did it for her. Before pulling away, her fingers caressed the back of Nydia's neck one last time, taking in the sensation of the smooth skin and the heavenly texture of her hair. She felt every muscle in her groin twitch in excitement.

"We have to stop," Jo said.

"Why?" Nydia asked with a slight whine and a pout that made her look even more adorable.

"Because, if we don't, I'm not going to want to stop."

"Then don't." Nydia's eyes were half closed, and her lips a touch apart as she leaned a little forward.

Jo wasn't sure if it was a conscious move or not, but as Jo stared at her, Nydia's tongue peeked out to moisten her lips. If she was trying for the part of seductress, she was doing a great job. Jo's heart felt ready to beat out of her chest.

"Nydia, are you —"

"If you ask me if I'm sure about this, I may have to do something drastic to you. I've never been surer of anything in my life. I want you, Jo. In every way. We've waited long enough. I need to show you how I feel about you. Words would fail me if I tried to say it."

"I feel the same way. You are the most amazing and beautiful woman I have ever met, in mind and soul. Not only in your looks." Jo laid her hand on the softness of Nydia's cheek. "But don't think you're not beautiful on the outside as well." She caressed the cheek with the back of her fingers, memorizing the sensation. The heat from Nydia's face was penetrating Jo's skin.

"It's been so long since I believed anything close to that about me. My mother was the only one who said it, and that I trusted meant it."

"Then I've been remiss. That is something you'll have to get used to hearing from me because I intend to tell you every day."

"Come inside. I need you," Nydia said, leaning her forehead on Jo's shoulder.

"Yeah, that would probably make sense. I'm sure your neighbors don't need to see," Jo said, her voice husky.

Nydia let out a nervous laugh. "Yeah, there is that, too."

Jo met Nydia by the passenger door, took her hand, and brought it to her lips. "Lead the way, my love," she said against the skin.

Jo didn't let go of Nydia's hand until she needed to unlock the door. Nydia managed the key, opened the door, and pulled Jo to her. Jo's back was to the door and her hands sought purchase while Nydia began kissing her senseless. Before Jo could think, her shirt was out of her pants and Nydia's fingers slid over her bare skin. Jo's knees started to buckle. She pulled the roaming hands away, trying to get a hold of her senses. Jo wasn't used to feeling so out of control. But with Nydia it was right.

Jo took a deep breath. "I love you, Nydia Rogers. You take my breath away and fill my heart."

Nydia smiled as her eyes glistened with tears.

As one fell, Jo reached out and brushed it away with her thumb. She placed a kiss over the trail. "Don't cry, please. I can't stand it."

Nydia looked deep into Jo's eyes, and Jo opened her soul for Nydia to see. She fell into Jo's embrace and clenched the back of her shirt. It felt as if Nydia was holding on for her life. Everything seemed perfect, and she wanted Nydia to feel safe in her arms.

After a moment, Nydia loosened her grip and whispered, "Let me show you how much I love you." She held out her hand.

Jo took it and her fingers entwined with Nydia's as they went up the stairs. Jo planned on spending the entire night expressing her love to Nydia.

***

They entered the bedroom still holding hands. Jo pulled Nydia into her and their bodies melded together. Jo's mouth sought out Nydia's, and Nydia sensed a consuming need build within her. Without letting her go, Nydia backed up until her knees hit the side of the bed. Jo reached out and undid Nydia's shirt. The slow movement was making her overheat, but Nydia felt the cool air of the room hit her overheated skin.

Jo pushed the shirt back off her shoulders and skimmed her fingertips down the length of Nydia's arm.

Nydia felt light-headed when Jo's fingers met her naked skin and glided along until she reached the clasp of Nydia's bra.

"Please—?" Jo asked.

Nydia heard her take in a deep breath. "God, yes, anything," She said. Her voice was a mere whisper.

The undergarment hit the floor as she finished speaking. Nydia shivered when she felt Jo's touch on her hip. With a gentle caress, Jo's hands started at her waist and, in a slow motion, she made her way up to the swell of Nydia's breasts. Nydia grew goosebumps form as Jo's fingers came to a rest on the crest of each breast, and then her hands covered them. The wetness in her groin began to slicken her thighs.

"You are as stunning outside as you are inside," Jo said, sealing the declaration with a kiss at the top of Nydia's right breast. "You have a beautiful soul and a body of equal splendor." Her head moved as she did the same to the left one.

Jo looked deep into Nydia's eyes, her hands kneading the breasts she held.

Nydia's breath hitched when, with an agonizing slowness, Jo began to slip her hands down, unding the button and zipper of her pants.

Jo's hand reached in, and ran her fingers through Nydia's now moist curls. "Please let me show you how much I love you."

Nydia saw the full essence of her love. "I think I may explode if you don't. Touch me and you'll see how much I need and love you."

Jo let her mouth move down to Nydia's light brown areola as her other hand slid along the planes of her stomach, and around her pelvis to reach her naked flank. Nydia's clit twitched and she threw her head back and moaned. Jo's fingers slid under the front of her panties and into her damp, hot folds.

With a restraint Nydia didn't know Jo could possess, she gently bathed a nipple with her slippery tongue, suckling lightly. Jo took her time, treating it with adoration as it rose. Jo gently blew across the erect nipple and Nydia shuddered.

"God, Jo. I'm so excited it hurts. I am so wet for you. Can you feel it?"

"I can feel it, and it's all for me, isn't it?"

"Yes. Yes. I've never been so wet."

"I love you so much, Nydia. Lay down, I want to feel your body under me, so I can watch you as you come, over and over again," Jo said as Nydia pulled her onto the bed.

"You may make me come right now." Nydia leaned up for another deep passionate kiss as her hands ran over Jo's shirt. "Please. I want to feel your skin. Take it off." Nydia's hands shook with excitement and anticipation. She could barely refrain from pulling the shirt off herself. However, she wanted to revel in the sight of Jo undressing, stripping for her enjoyment.

Jo surprised her by standing and slowly removing all her clothes. The last piece fell to the floor and Jo stood before her naked, her arms held wide. She oozed confidence and self-assurance.

Nydia reached out and softly caressed the full breasts before her.

She had desired to hold them, to feel them, since her first encounter with Jo.

Jo laid down next to Nydia and turned the bedside lamp off so that only the lights from outside illuminated the room. Jo's love radiated off her, and Nydia drank it in like a drowning woman. Her only wish was that she could express it just as equally.

Jo pulled the covers over them. "Let me feel you next to me, under me. I want to taste you." She pulled them together so the whole length of their bodies seemed to meld into one. The kiss they shared was full of passion, and the promise of a night full of love and worship of each other.

Chapter Twenty-one

NYDIA WOKE AS THE light of the clear morning sun filtered through her eyelids. The pressure of Jo's body against her back gave Nydia a sense of comfort and safety. She let out a contented sigh. She saw a new reality that she never imagined for herself, one of deep and all-consuming emotions. The love she held for Jo was more than she had ever known before. There was a rightness about it, of being home, safe, and cared about. A sense of being loved wholly and unconditionally. Jo's hand reached around her waist and pulled her closer.

Jo's hand reached around Nydia's waist and pulled her closer. Jo's hot breath tickled her ear and made her shiver. "Waking up and holding you is my new favorite alarm clock." Jo laid a kiss on the back of Nydia's neck. "I never want to leave this bed."

Nydia rolled over and came face to face with the woman she now believed held her heart. "I would agree, but I have work to get to."

A tear came to Jo's eye and slowly made its way down her cheek. Nydia reached out and brushed it away with the pad of her thumb. "I hope that is a tear of happiness."

Jo leaned in for another kiss. "Don't worry, it is. I can't describe how happy I am."

Nydia smiled. "I have the same feeling." She recognized she was no longer the broken person her father and brothers had created. Nydia knew her mother would have supported her relationship with Jo. She took solace in that idea.

Jo moved in and pressed her lips against Nydia's. Jo's tongue caressed her bottom lip while her hand cupped Nydia's breast.

Nydia stopped Jo's roaming hand by placing her own over it and let out a deep sigh. "As much as I would love to continue where we left off, I need to go to work."

Jo let out a loud breath and moved her hand away, touching their lips together one more time before she drew back. "Okay, I'll behave, but don't expect me to be happy about it."

Nydia giggled. "I won't. I'm not any happier than you, but work calls." She slapped Jo's bare butt cheek as she got out of bed and put on her robe. "Go shower and I'll go make coffee."

***

Nydia strode through the ER bay doors later, more content then she had ever been. *It's all Jo's doing. God, I love her so much.*

"What's got into you today," Trudy asked with a smile, "or should I say who?"

Nydia almost spit her coffee out through her nose. She had to hold her hand up while she snorted to keep the liquid in. "Geez. Could you be crasser?" Nydia wiped off her chin. "Don't pretend for a second that you don't have a perfectly good clue what's going on. After all, you've been praying for this whole thing for months now."

Trudy grinned. "Guilty as charged." She let out a small laugh. "I'm just so happy for you guys. You deserve this. You especially. With all the bullshit you've had to put up with over the years, a great wad of sappy love and sex is exactly what you deserve."

"'A wad of love and sex? Really, you're going to go with that?" Nydia leaned on the counter of the nurses' station and they both laughed.

Trudy gave her an awkward hug over the counter. "Yes, I will. It suits you both. I assume your big, stoic, teddy bear of a cop has a similar goofy grin on her face?" Trudy walked around the counter.

Nydia looked around to see that no one was close enough to hear them. "I think so," she said in a hushed tone. "Well, let's say she better, otherwise I'm in this predicament all by myself, and that's just too freaking scary."

"I'm positive Jo does. You two make quite the couple. The way she looks at you tells me she feels the same way you do right now."

Nydia looked down for a moment. "I hope so. This is all so new to me. So beyond anything I've ever felt for anyone before. Even my mother."

Trudy took hold of Nydia's hand. "I know, honey, and from what you've told me about her and what I remember, I know that your mother would be ecstatic for you and Jo. Fuck the rest of them."

"Shh, language, please." Nydia grinned. "Seriously though, thanks for saying that. I've been trying to convince myself of that all morning."

Trudy smiled and gave Nydia's hand one more squeeze before letting go. "Nydia, we grew up on the same block. I remember your mother. How her eyes lit up whenever you were together. Her face beamed when she saw you get off the school bus. Those were the only times I saw her smile like that. I know she loved you and would want you to be happy. She wouldn't care that it was a woman who made you this joyful. She'd only care that you were, and she would embrace her. Jo loves you with her whole heart and soul. I can see that, so I'm positive your mom would love her too."

"Disgusting."

Nydia jumped. Looking over her shoulder, Nydia wasn't surprised to see Dr. Goddard. "Is there something in particular I can help you with, Dr. Goddard, or are you just in the habit of insinuating yourself into other people's conversations?" Nydia gave him a disdainful look. Out of the corner of her eye she saw Trudy trying not to smirk. Nydia decided he wasn't worth her effort today, so she tried to keep a stern face.

"It's bad enough they let your perverted type into this profession, and even give you a role of authority, but to have you spreading your filth and debauched life for anyone to see, or hear, is more than decent people should be subjected to."

"By 'my type' are you referring to women in general or lesbians in particular? Because neither one is any of your business, Dr. Goddard."

"Both, and they are very much my business. Your being here takes a job away from a man. Men who support their wives, not as some hobby as you women do."

"Well, since, as you've pointed out, I'm gay, and therefore not waiting for a husband, this is my job and the rest is, as I just said, none of your damn business. It's time you moved out of the Dark Ages, Dr. Goddard, and joined the majority of America who has come to realize that neither being a woman, nor a lesbian, is a basis for having me stoned to death."

"Death would be a welcome reprieve from the likes of you people. I would personally see that you, and individuals similar to you, who spread your depraved morals like a pestilence, were gone from this earth. Cleansing the world of the likes of you would be a benefit to humanity. I, for one, would do anything to protect my family and these patients from people as sinful as you. Eventually, everyone will see that women, dykes, and sodomites are incapable of this kind of work. Your minds are too weak, your morals depraved. You're nothing more than pedophiles and rapists, and someday it will cost some poor individual their life. Better you be taken care of now before you do more damage.

Professionally or physically makes no matter, but I will see you destroyed."

"Goddard." Nydia's face turned deep red as she gave up all pretense of respect and civility. "That sounded like a threat. Do you want to reconsider those words? Because this is the last time I will put up with this behavior. I will be filing a formal report with Dr. Stephenson. You can explain yourself to him."

Dr. Goddard sputtered, but started to answer. "I—"

"Unless your answer is yes, then, shut up. As head of this department, I strongly suggest you get out of my sight. I will be notifying Dr. Stephenson that I am requesting your actions be investigated. How dare you threaten me." She all but shouted at him. She began to shake with anger. Out of the corner of her eye she saw Trudy speaking into the phone.

"I was merely stating facts."

"Bullshit. You just stood there, in front of a witness no less, and threatened to destroy me either, as you said, 'professionally or physically.' You're lucky that this may only cost you your job. But you will be the one who suffers here, not me. I guarantee it. Now, I suggest you stay out of my sight and don't come anywhere near me unless you have an issue with a patient."

Nydia turned and made her way toward her office. She didn't think she could look at anyone at the moment. Before she had a chance to open the door, she startled when a hand rested on her back and began rubbing it. She opened her eyes, not realizing she had closed them. Trudy looked at her and her concern and reassurance were evident to Nydia.

"Nydia, he's gone, honey. I sent him in with a patient. I called the Nursing Supervisor, according to procedure, and she's calling Dr. Stephenson. I called Jo, too. Dr. Goddard scared even me, so I thought she should know. Everything will be okay. Come on. Let's get you out of the hallway."

Nydia realized Trudy mentioned procedures. She had things to deal with as well. She had her own guidelines and standards of operation to follow. She started to open the door but heard a commotion behind her. She turned to see what was happening and saw Dr. Stephenson coming down the hall toward her. Nydia stepped into her office and held the door open for him. The next moment she felt his arms engulf her into a close hug. At that instant, she knew this was what a father's love felt like. She buried her face into his shoulder, smelling his faint cologne as she took a deep calming breath.

After a few seconds, Nydia felt her demeanor returning to normal enough to deal with the current situation. She let go and took a step back from him, tears she refused to let fall were shining in her eyes.

"What the hell happened?" he asked, looking at Trudy. "I got a call from the Nursing Supervisor. She said you had a confrontation with Dr. Goddard and that he threatened you."

Nydia saw the concern in Trudy's face and stretched out a hand toward her. After Trudy took it, Nydia took a deep calming breath and began to explain what happened. Her shaking voice was the only sign of her distress. "I'm not sure where to start."

Trudy let go and interrupted on her behalf. Nydia was grateful. She didn't know if she could explain without breaking down.

"Dr. Rogers and I were talking to each other, alone. Dr. Goddard stepped in and started spouting such vile vitriol I was shocked. He verbally attacked Dr. Rogers, saying the most disgusting things about her, then he threatened her career and her. To be honest, Dr. Stephenson, I'm still in shock. I've never seen such hatred that close up from a fellow staff member."

Nydia listened to Trudy as she relayed the facts and thought, *That's exactly what it felt like. He actually wanted me dead.* A cold chill traveled down her spine. *What if Trudy hadn't been here? What if he had decided to get physical?*

Dr. Stephenson looked at Nydia with deep concern, his lips pressing together. "Is this true?"

"Yes." Nydia swallowed a lump in her throat.

"I'll have this investigated. I can promise you, Nydia, I will handle this. In the meantime, he won't have the ability to be anywhere near you. As of now, he's suspended, pending review. Don't worry about anything here. Your safety and well-being are my primary concern right now. Let me go talk to Dr. Goddard. I want to get this started as soon as possible," he said before stepping out of the room.

Nydia heard sirens coming closer to the Emergency Bay and walked out to meet the ambulance.

"Nydia!"

Nydia looked up and was surprised to see Jo coming through behind the crew.

"Hey, can you take this one over?" Nydia asked Trent, the other doctor on staff, as he came up next to her.

"Sure, no problem. It's a basic case. I heard it called in."

Before she had a chance to think, Jo had her hand on Nydia's arm and was leading her back to the office. Once the door closed, Jo engulfed her in the protection of her arms and Nydia lost any control she had left.

***

"Shhh, honey, I've got you now. Nothing is going to happen. I'll keep you safe. I promise on my life."

Though her words were spoken in truth, Jo had never felt so scared, or as helpless as she did when she got the call from Trudy. Now, all Jo could do was hold Nydia close, whisper soothing words, and be strong and protect her. Jo felt Nydia's sobs deep in her own heart, and it hurt. She reassured her through gentle rubs along her back and held her tight.

After a light knock on the door, Dr. Stephenson poked his head in. "Is it okay to come in?"

Jo motioned him in.

"Nydia, I want you to go home. Take the next few days off while I get this situation investigated," he said as he softly came into the room.

Jo wasn't sure Nydia was even aware of him at the moment.

"I'll take her to my place. My family and I will be there for her, always."

Chapter Twenty-two

JO STOPPED IN THE driveway and put the car in park. "Nydia, honey, we're home. Nydia, are you okay, sweetheart?"

"Huh? Yeah, I'm fine," Nydia said as she turned to face Jo while she wiped at her face with her hands.

Jo caught sight of the tearstains on her cheeks, and knew she was far from okay. She got out and went around the car. "Come on. Mom probably has some nice, hot food on." She held out her hand to assist Nydia out of the car. *I hope she does. I've never felt so lost in my life. I have no idea how to fix this. Hell, Mom's been fixing it my whole life. Now, I hope she can do the same for Nydia.*

Cassandra opened the door as they approached. "What's the matter? What happened? Are you okay?" She rubbed her hands together and a slight tremble cracked her voice. "You sounded upset on the phone. Are you hurt? Is Duncan?"

"I'm okay Mom. It's Nydia. She had a confrontation at work and her boss thought she should take a day or so off. I'm sorry. I didn't mean to worry you about me."

"Never mind that, what happened? What kind of confrontation?" Cassandra put an arm around Nydia's shoulder. "Come inside, dear."

"It's a bit complicated. My concern was to get her home," Jo said as she focused all her attention on Nydia.

Cassandra took over and ushered Nydia to the front room, talking to her in the gentle tone she usually reserved for Jo and Ellie when they were sick. "Shh, dear. We're here for you. You're surrounded by love and family here."

Nydia's arms flew around Cassandra. Jo's heart broke for the woman she loved as she seemed to lose what control she had left. Jo held back her own tears as Nydia buried her face in the crook of Cassandra's neck. Her body was wracked with sobs. Cassandra could barely hold them both up, so Jo helped guide them to the couch and got them settled in.

Cassandra leaned back against the couch cushions, holding Nydia in her arms. Nydia cried and was barely able to catch her breath.

"My poor child, that's it, let it all go," Cassandra said in a gentle, soothing tone.

Jo felt helpless for the first time since she was a child.

"Honey, can you go get Nydia something to drink? Give us some time to talk." She winked at Jo to let her know she would take care of Nydia, and to give her room to help Nydia heal a little.

"Sure, sure thing, Mom, I'll make some tea," Jo said, turning and heading to the kitchen, relieved to have something to do.

***

"It's okay, sweetie. No one's going to hurt you, Nydia, not anymore. You're safe here," Cassandra said.

After a few minutes, Nydia lost the energy to keep crying. She was exhausted. The only thing holding her upright was Cassandra.

Cassandra reached behind her, pulled several tissues free from the box on the end table, and placed them in Nydia's hand. "Here, sweetie, try and dry your eyes. Give your nose a good blow, too. You'll feel better, I promise."

Nydia sat up, grateful for Cassandra's care. The expression on her face reminded Nydia of her mother.

As if reading her mind, Cassandra said, "I can't tell you the number of times I sat with my daughters like this. Now it's my turn with my new daughter."

Nydia wiped the tears off her face, and blew her nose before laying her head on Cassandra's shoulder, letting the woman soothe her bruised soul. She must have fallen asleep because she woke when Cassandra spoke again.

"Honey, do you think you're up for some tea now?"

"Is Jo still here?" Nydia asked in a small voice.

Jo came around the corner and sat next to her, Nydia melted into her arms. "I'm right here, sweetheart. I never left. I will never leave."

Without letting go of Jo, Nydia stretched her hand out to Cassandra, who took it. "Thank you for being here, Cassandra."

"Call me Mom. You're a part of this family now, and I hope I helped."

"Thank you, you did," Nydia said with a tired smile. She looked at Jo, her face growing serious as a crinkle appeared on her forehead. "I remember now, at least most of it, I think."

Jo placed a tender kiss on her lover's lips. Nydia pushed away without letting go. "Remember what?"

"Barbara Donnelly, I have to tell you about Barbara. I know her."

"You what? How do you know her?"

"Barbara and I grew up together. We weren't close, but she lived around the corner. We had the same bus stop."

"Why didn't you remember this before?" Jo ran her fingers through her hair. She didn't want to upset Nydia, but she needed answers.

"I don't know. Maybe I pushed those bad memories away, buried them, and her along with it."

"Why do you think you would do that?"

"I was just a kid at the time. We went to school together until junior high. Her father..." Nydia let out a deep sigh. "He beat her, and he was vicious about it. There seemed to be a new bruise every few days. It was awful."

"Come on, let's sit back. You can explain it to me. Mom, would you mind giving us some time?"

"Of course not. I'll go put some of the leftover stew on the stove. You can have it when you're ready," Cassandra said as she stood and walked out of the room.

"So, can you tell me about it?"

"Yeah, I'm ready to. I think I need to explain a couple of things to you."

"Okay. Take your time." Jo pulled a notepad off the coffee table. "Do you mind if I take notes? Only about Barbara, though. I may need them later for her case."

"Sure, I guess so. I want to tell you more than that, though. I want to share my story too, because you can't understand one without the other. At least I don't think so, not to me."

"Her name was Barbara O'Keeffe then. We weren't friends but were on the same bus. She was a grade ahead of me. I lost track of her when she went to middle school. I heard she dropped out in her junior year of high school. The rumor was she got pregnant."

"So, she had a history of being abused?"

"Yeah, her father would beat her, what seemed like, several times a week, and he wasn't very good at making sure no one could see the bruises. But back in those days, you didn't really ask. Plus, at the time, I had a good deal going on in my life," Nydia said through a lump in her throat.

"My mom died a few years before I realized what was happening to her, and by then my father had started on me. He was more of an emotional abuser though. The physical stuff he left for Richard and sometimes Stevie Jr, would join in. Mom died during an argument with my dad. Stevie Jr. and I were hiding in his bedroom. We did that when they were at it. We would hide in the closet and I would hold him until it was safe to come out. It was one of the bigger fights. I heard them arguing and what sounded like things breaking. I tried to keep him from crying too much. Then it got quiet. Anyway, according to the police there that night, Mom slipped and hit her head.

"Barbara was in the same kind of situation. I remember one instance when her father met her when she got off the bus. She looked so scared. He grabbed her arm and dragged her inside. She cried the whole time."

"What about her mother?" Jo asked as she scribbled in her pad.

"They were divorced, from what I remember. I heard from my dad that she was a drunk and slept around. How much of that was true, I can't say."

"Do you know what happened to Barbara after she left?"

Nydia looked at her hands clasped on her lap. "No. I have to be honest. I never thought about it."

Jo put her hand over Nydia's. "There's nothing to be sorry about. You were just a kid dealing with your own problems." She looked down at her notes. "Was there any word of the baby? From what we know, she doesn't have any children."

"I heard some rumors about an abortion or miscarriage, but nothing more than that. I'm sorry, Jo." Nydia was unable to meet Jo's gaze.

Jo lifted Nydia's chin up so their eyes met. "Stop apologizing, Nydia. What others do has nothing to do with you. We'll catch her husband, and if we need to, whoever's helping him as well."

Chapter Twenty-three

JO LAY IN BED, wide-awake at three-twenty. She could hear the gentle sound of Nydia's breathing next to her. It was hard to believe that the emotional events at the hospital and her mom's house, were only two days before.

They had spent the day at her mom's. After dinner, Nydia told them all she wanted was to go home and sleep. Nydia was exhausted by the time they got to her house, but when Jo said good night at the door, Nydia put her hand on Jo's chest, right over her heart.

"Stay with me."

Jo placed a soft kiss on Nydia's lips and wrapped her in her arms. "For as long as you need and want me to," she whispered in Nydia's ear.

Jo remembered feeling Nydia's body relax into her as she wrapped her arms around Jo's waist, and laying her head on her shoulder. After that, Jo had no power to refuse as Nydia led her upstairs, never letting go of her hand. She stayed for both nights and had called in for time off at work.

I never want to let go. For us to always need and be there for each other would make my world. Emotionally, mentally, and physically I want her, and I hope she'll always need and want me. For here and now though, I'll do everything in my power to protect her and keep her happy. Jo closed her eyes, lulled back to sleep by the sound of Nydia next to her.

***

Nydia walked through the ER entrance at six forty-five sharp. It felt harder than it should have, but after the incident two days before, she didn't want to give anyone the impression that her ability to do her job was diminished. As she walked toward her office, and past the nurses' station, she heard the whispering. With the worst part over, she walked with her head held high. However, the complicated part wouldn't be done until the issue with Dr. Goddard was taken care of. At least she wouldn't have to deal with him until then, since he wasn't allowed back to work until it was. She set her travel mug on her desk and let out a deep sigh.

Trudy looked through the door Nydia had left ajar. "Hi. How are you holding up?" she asked, concern in her voice.

"Come on in. Close the door."

They each took a seat.

"Honestly? About as well as can be expected. When we left, Jo took me to her place. Her mother was a big help. She is a wonderful woman. Jo and I also had a long talk about my past. They both make me feel so safe and loved." Her mind drifted to waking up with Jo this morning. She enjoyed the feeling of love and security so much so that she didn't want to get out of bed. Now she felt refreshed. She hadn't felt that in many years.

"I'm glad to hear it. I was worried about you after you left. I'm happy to hear you opened up to Jo. Does it make you feel better?"

"Yeah, it does. Thanks for the caring, Trudy. I really appreciate it. You're the best friend I have and you mean a lot to me. I'm sure I don't tell you that enough."

Trudy wiped at the corner of her eye. "Now look what you did. You made me get all teary. Don't get me all sappy. I know how hard it's been for you over the years, but now you have that wonderful pile of gorgeousness to love you, and for you to love her." Trudy pushed herself out of the chair. "So, as a medical professional, I order you to live happily ever after. If you don't, I call dibs on her."

"And what would your husband have to say about that?"

"Okay, fine. You can keep her. Suck all the fun out of it." Trudy gave Nydia a frown that lacked any sign of sincerity.

Nydia smiled and giggled. "I intend to. For as long as possible." A lump formed in her chest for a moment as she realized how much she truly meant that statement. She wanted to spend the rest of her life with Jo. Before Nydia had a chance to think on it more, the phone rang. Trudy picked it up.

"Oh, Dr. Stephenson. Hello. It's Nurse Swenson." Trudy looked at her. "Yes, I'll tell her right away. Thank you. Bye."

"Guess this means he's made a decision," Nydia said in a quiet tone. She heard the insecurity in her own voice and was disappointed in herself.

"He asked if you could meet him in the Boardroom."

Nydia stood up straight and squared her shoulders. Today, a call there could mean only one thing. The Board was deciding on a course of action. "I'll be back as soon as I can. Have Dr. Williams cover the ER until then. If anything big comes in, page me and I'll see if I can get free." As she walked away, she looked over her shoulder. "Wish me luck."

"You don't need luck, Nydia. You did nothing wrong. Remember that."

"Thanks."

Nydia let Trudy's words sink in as she made her way to the west wing elevator. She took a few minutes to think about the events leading up to this meeting. *Trudy was right. I only acted in a professional manner with Dr. Goddard. If anything, I bent over backwards to make allowances for his behavior.* In no time, Nydia was knocking on the Boardroom door.

"Come in."

She walked in and was met with the full Board and Dr. Stephenson, sitting around the conference table. Nydia swallowed to try to relieve her sudden case of nerves and sat in the empty chair nearest the door.

Dr. Stephenson offered her a subtle smile when she looked in his direction. She relaxed a little bit and gave her attention to the President of the Board, Peter Jeffries. She had spoken to him at various hospital social events, but that was the limit of her interactions with him.

"Good morning, Dr. Rogers. I'm assuming you know why we're here today," Jeffries said.

"I believe so. Yes." She rested her hands on the table, trying to look calm. But she felt the sweat begin to form on the back of her neck and resisted the urge to wipe it.

"Good, let's get started. It's been reported to us that the incident the other day was not the first time Dr. Goddard has had a confrontation with you of this sort. Is that true?"

"Yes, that is true. Recently there was an incident where he grabbed me physically and verbally assaulted me." Nydia wasn't entirely comfortable making the accusation, but she knew it was time for his behavior to come to light. Jo and her mother had shown her that she needed to stand up for herself against such actions.

"At that time, did he threaten you to the extent he did in this incident?" Jeffries asked.

"No. At least not verbally, though physically he grabbed me, but didn't threaten. In that instance, he said I was an evil heathen not worthy of working here, and he would have my job taken away. He also threatened the job of the police detective I was with at the time when she intervened in his physical assault," Nydia said in a calm but firm voice. She refused to feel on the defensive. What Goddard did was wrong, and she would stand by that. She was strong enough to stop feeling like a victim of men like Goddard and her family.

"Was this a pattern between you and Dr. Goddard?" a younger Board member asked.

"No. There had never been anything to this degree. However, Dr. Goddard has spent quite some time trying to undermine my authority, especially when I try to review his work. On several occasions it was brought to the attention of Dr. Stephenson by Dr. Goddard."

Jeffries turned to Dr. Stephenson. "Is that right, Dr. Stephenson?"

"Yes. My office has logged numerous complaints over the last few years, but after review, each was deemed unfounded. I spoke to Dr. Goddard after his last report and told him that if it persisted, it would be looked at as violations of our harassment policies."

Jeffries made a notation on the notepad in front of him. "And you've had time to look into this particular incident?"

"Yes. I've spent the interim time interviewing the witnesses and recording their statements. I drafted the formal report and conclusions. A copy was issued to each of you yesterday afternoon."

"Those contained the recommendation you presented to us here earlier today?" Jeffries asked

Jim glanced at Nydia. "Yes."

"Does anyone have any more questions?" Jeffries looked at each of the other members. When no one spoke up, he turned back to Nydia. "Thank you for your cooperation, Dr. Rogers. We have your statement on record, and we will most likely make a determination today."

"Thank you, sir." Nydia stood up and pushed her chair in. She closed the door behind her as she left, relieved to know that Dr. Goddard's future at the hospital was not in her hands.

***

Nydia was in the doctors' lounge trying to take a minute to re-center herself when Trudy walked in.

"So how did it go?"

Nydia didn't have the energy to rehash the event with her and hospital policy let her avoid it. "About as well as to be expected, I can't say more than that. Trudy, would you mind if I took a few minutes in here alone? I need some room right now. I just want to relax on the couch and have a cup of coffee. I don't have the energy to take it back to my office."

"Sure, Nydia, anything you need. I'll try and keep the rest of the staff away."

"Thanks. It's nothing personal."

"I know that. Don't worry about me right now. Take care of you for a change."

It had been a draining couple of days, but Nydia refused to give Dr. Goddard any more power over her. She decided no one would be allowed to treat her like that again. She was done with it. *Never again,* she thought as she put her feet up.

Several hours later, after a busy day in the ER, Dr. Stephenson found her in her office, sitting with her head back, and nursing another cup of coffee.

"Hi. How are you holding up?" he asked as he sat down in the chair across from her.

She lifted her head up. "As well as can be expected."

"That well, huh? I thought I would come down and let you know the Board's decision. It will become formal later today, but I was given permission to tell you unofficially. I explained it would be to the benefit of the department if it was off your mind."

"So, what happened?" Nydia leaned forward and put her mug on the desk.

"Dr. Goddard will be given two choices based on the Boards' determination. If he is smart, he will figure out it's in his best interest to hand in his resignation. Otherwise, he will be fired."

Nydia let out the breath she was holding. "It's over, then."

"Yes. He'll be allowed to collect his possessions, but then he'll be gone."

"How did he take it?"

Jim's face darkened. "He didn't take it well. All I can say is that security escorted him out of the room and will supervise the visit to remove his belongings. Nydia, I'm sorry that you had to be put in this position and go through this."

"It's okay. In the long run, I think, in a strange way, he did me a favor. I've come to realize that I've let people like him control my life for too long."

"I'm glad you can find something positive out of this. I truly am," Dr. Stephenson said as he stood up. "You're lucky to have that woman in your life. She looked like she was torn between demanding Goddard's head on a platter and making sure you were taken care of."

"Jo. Her name is Jo. Sometime, I'd like to introduce you to her. I think you would like her."

"I'm sure I would," Jim said as he left the room.

A burden lifted off her shoulders. She reached in her pocket, pulled out her phone, and hit Jo's number. Maybe she would be free after work. A large smile graced her face as the idea struck her heart.

Chapter Twenty-four

AFTER TAKING A WELL-deserved weekend off to spend with Nydia, Jo sat at her desk. Quiet time at Nydia's relaxed both of them after the incident with Goddard. Although it had been three weeks since his firing, Nydia was still anxious. Now, Jo spent most of the morning wondering how Nydia's day was going.

Last night, they set up tentative plans for tonight that she looked forward to. Now, though, she needed to take her mind off Nydia. She had to focus on work. She looked at Duncan as he was hanging up the phone.

He gave her a broad smile. "We finally have a lead on Donnelly."

"Great. What do we got?" If Jo could close this case, it would make her day. After the story Nydia told her, Jo wanted to give Barbara this victory.

"He's holed up in one of the campgrounds over in Smith Point County Park. He's using a RV with fake plates. One of the park rangers noticed the guy hanging around matched the description of Todd Donnelly we released to the other agencies. They're keeping an eye on it for us. I asked that they stand down until we arrived."

"Are we ready to go?" Jo was pulling her coat off the back of her chair.

"Right behind you."

***

Smith Point County Park in the off-season had little advantage for the group of officers that showed up. It was a small strip of Fire Island with the Atlantic Ocean on one side and part of the Great South Bay on the other. The only cover it gave them was the dunes, sea grass, and a few scrub pines. With the late fall weather, only about a half-a-dozen campers were in the area.

Since the park was County land, Duncan had notified the County Police. Unfortunately, their SWAT team and most units were busy dealing with an incident further up island, and thus, were unavailable. They were given the go-ahead. They had uniform back up and a K-9 unit, but that was it.

The ranger in charge told them Todd was alone, so Jo wasn't worried about hostages. Todd didn't have a firearm registered to him, and his wife didn't think he owned one. However, she had to worry about the safety of the other campers and her co-workers, as well as the potential that Todd was desperate enough to try suicide by cop.

Before they arrived, the rangers evacuated what few campers there were in the immediate vicinity. At the back of the RV, Jo and her team of two uniforms were in position at the entrance side of his camper. Duncan and his team on the other side. The remaining uniforms were in the dunes. They let Jo know through her earpiece that they had a good line of sight to the RV door and front windows.

Jo didn't hear their perp moving around inside. At the back window she peeped through the partially opened curtain and she could see through the front. Todd was sitting at a table on the driver side. Moving from the back bumper, Jo made her way to the side door with a uniformed officer behind her, and another behind him. They all stayed low to avoid the windows.

She knew Duncan would be sticking to the plan. He and his uniformed partner would be moving up the other side to try to reach the front window. If their luck held, Todd wouldn't see any of them and would remain where he was.

Jo got into place by the door with her gun drawn. As Duncan gave the signal in her earpiece, she flung the door open and, in a swift motion went inside, gun first yelling "Police. Don't move." Jo zeroed in on Todd sitting at the table, one hand under the table the other draped along the back of the bench seat. "Police. Todd, don't think of moving." She kept an eye on the arm held under the table, as another officer came in behind her and took up position next to her but slightly behind. "That barking you're hearing is a very angry police dog waiting for a chance to get at you. One word, one movement, and he comes in. We have the camper surrounded. So, right now you're not getting out of here unless I say so. It's up to you, Todd, whether it's on your own two feet or not."

Todd glared at them. His face was red, but he stayed put.

Jo was grateful he was at least that smart. "Very slowly place your hands behind your head, fingers interlocked."

"You'll regret this. You don't know who you're messing with."

Todd's voice was steady and calm as he followed her directions.

"I know exactly who you are, Todd, and what you've done. I'm going to make sure you go to prison for it."

"I'll never see the inside of a cell, let alone prison."

Jo hoped he wasn't planning something stupid. "Place your head face down on the table."

As Todd followed her commands, Jo called out to the others who came in. Now that he was covered, she wasn't as worried about too many people in the crowded camper.

"Madison," she said to the officer behind her. "Take up my position while I pat him down and cuff him. Everyone else stay close, but I don't want you too bunched up here until it's clear."

Madison moved in so she had a clear line. "I got him, Detective."

"Thanks." Jo holstered her gun and slowly made her way over to Todd, making sure she didn't cross Madison's sight line. She clasped his hands in one of hers.

"Stand up gradually and step out." Jo used her free hand to direct him up and out.

Once he was on his feet, she cuffed him. With the final click, she began patting his body from his neck down. "Anything on you I should know about?"

Todd stayed silent.

Duncan came into the RV and whistled as Jo brought out the Ruger from under the table. "There's a catch for it under here. He probably had his hand on it the entire time." Jo swallowed hard, thinking how things could have ended differently than they had.

"Lucky he's at least smart enough he didn't use it," Duncan said as he took the gun from her.

Jo let out a low whistle. "I'm impressed, Todd. That is certainly an expensive piece of machinery you have there. I would think that is way above your pay scale." Jo leaned toward Todd while looking at Duncan. "Maybe it was a gift from a friend. Perhaps the same one who helped you get set up in this nice cozy nest?" Jo said in a low voice.

Todd turned his head and glared at her. "I want my lawyer. His card's in my front pocket."

"Well, that is certainly convenient," Duncan said with a raised eyebrow as he finished securing his pistol back in its holster.

Jo read Todd his Miranda Rights as she led him down the stairs and to the nearest cruiser. "Are you sure you don't have anything to say?" she asked before ducking his head to put him into it.

“As I already told you, the only thing I want from you is my lawyer,” he said once he was sitting down. He glowered up at her.

Jo slammed the door shut and hit the top of the car with her hand, giving the officer inside permission to drive off. She stared as the Crime Scene Unit van pulled up by the camper. She mulled over what happened. *Who the hell is helping him? There is no way he thought to be this prepared on his own.* Once the patrol car pulled away, she went to their own car. Duncan joined her and stood next to the passenger door.

“I don’t like his smug attitude. It tells me he thinks he has this covered,” he said.

Jo looked at him over the top of the car.

“I agree. I was just wondering if he has something up his sleeve, or maybe someone.” As she watched the car drive down the beach road, she was already trying to make connections between Todd, his ability to evade them, and how he got his hands on an RV. She contemplated the situation to herself. *How did Todd go undetected for as long as he did, especially with the park rangers patrolling as much as they did? Was he here the entire time they’d been looking for him? If not here, then where? If he had been here, someone with pull was helping. Otherwise, the rangers would have reported him earlier. He couldn’t hide in this thing that long without notice. He’s been one step ahead.*

“I don’t think we’re going to like where this goes. I think he had a lot of help. That gun didn’t just fall into his lap, and based on his financial records, I doubt he could afford to buy it, even off the street.”

“I’m with you on that.”

“That’s what we get paid for, partner,” Jo said when they got in the car. She gave him a backhanded slap to his arm. “Let’s head out. We’re going to be spending a lot of time on this paperwork, and with a lawyer involved from the get-go, I’m sure we won’t be getting answers out of him any time soon.”

Chapter Twenty-five

JO AND DUNCAN STEPPED out of the station and into the evening summer air. It had been five hours of paperwork and arguing with Todd's attorney. They finally booked him at five-thirty, so being Friday, it took some BS on their part, but convinced his lawyer to waive the arraignment until Monday. Todd Donnelly was now spending the weekend in the county jail. They signed out for the night which now gave them two days to find out what was going on. Jo knew there had to be more to what was going on the surface, and Duncan had agreed.

Jo's cell phone rang. She reached for it, hoping it wasn't more work. Focusing on this case over the next two days had to be her priority. Jo was sorry that meant cancelling her Saturday plans with Nydia. "Powers here," she answered, not looking at the caller ID.

"Hi. It's me, did I interrupt anything?"

Jo smiled at the sound of Nydia's voice. "Hi me. How are you? The answer is no. Sorry about that. I was distracted." Nydia's laughter resonated through the phone and made Jo's smile grow bigger.

"I'm fine. I'm finishing at the hospital and was hoping it was possible you were free to meet up for some dinner."

"Can you hold on for a second?"

"For you, I will wait forever. How is that for an answer?" Nydia said with a slight lilt.

"Sounds like a perfect one to me. Just a sec." She looked at Duncan. "Nydia wants to meet up for dinner. Want to join us?"

"Sure. There's nothing more we can do tonight. Maddy and the kids are up island visiting her mother overnight. I was going to grab a bite and head there afterwards, so I'm up for it." Duncan grinned.

"Is it okay for Duncan to come?" Jo asked Nydia.

"Of course. He's always welcome. Want to meet at the Snack Bar?"

Jo smiled at the mention of her favorite restaurant. A good piece of pie would help pick up her mood. "Sure. Meet you there in about twenty minutes?"

"It's a date," Nydia said.

"Why, yes, it is."

"Goof. I'll see you then. I'm packed up and only need to log off."

"I can't wait. I love you, by the way." She didn't wait for Nydia to say it back before disconnecting the call. She was sure enough of Nydia's feelings to not need an answer.

"Come on. I'm starving."

"For her, or food?" Duncan smirked.

***

Jo enjoyed the Snack Bar. It was comfortable, and the people who worked there were some of the friendliest waitstaff she had come across. The diner looked about the same as when it opened in the early fifties, right down to the Formica tables, brown and rust floral carpet, and oldies music piped in over the hidden speakers. She relaxed as she and Duncan both nursed a craft beer.

Nydia slipped into the chair next to Jo. "Hi, guys." Nydia's hand rested on Jo's thigh under the table.

Jo smiled.

Duncan looked at her and then Nydia with a grin.

Jo winked at him, acknowledging her happiness.

"Did you guys order yet?" Nydia asked as she picked up a menu. "I'm starving. Work was non-stop today. We had a motor vehicle accident with three unrestrained victims."

"How did they make out?" Duncan asked.

Nydia's smile disappeared. "The first patient was bad off. His face plus the head injury were too much for our trauma level two, so we had to transport him to the university's level one trauma center. I'm surprised he even made it to Riverview, but he has a chance. Of the other two, we lost one as the bleeding was too extensive. She made it to us in time for us to call it, and the second one got off with a fractured leg." Nydia's shoulders slumped.

"I'm sure you did everything you could for them. I'm sorry it wasn't enough this time." Jo gave Nydia's leg a squeeze.

Duncan picked up a menu. "I'm sorry too. Okay. Change of subject, let's get our minds off work for two minutes. I'm starving, so let's order."

Peggy, one of the waitresses, stopped at their table. "Hi guys. Nice to see everyone today. So, what can I get you this evening?"

Jo handed her back the menu when they were all done ordering. "I hope we're done with work, for the day, at least. Today was one long ass day."

"What happened?" Nydia asked, her voice full of concern.

"We were able to get a break on Barbara Donnelly's husband Todd. We spent the day arresting and questioning him. He should be spending some time in jail at least until his arraignment Monday, maybe longer if his bail is set high enough. I doubt they will let him go on his own recognizance."

"Yup. Our guy Todd will be spending the night getting booked and making friends inside our lovely jail facility. I hope he misses dinner call," Duncan said with a broad grin.

"Todd Donnelly?" Nydia asked.

"Yeah. Why? I'm pretty sure he's not a friend of yours," Duncan said.

"No. His name sounds familiar, though."

"Really? I suppose Donnelly is a common enough name around here," Duncan said.

"No, it's more than that. I think my brother knew a Todd Donnelly when we were kids."

Jo looked at Duncan as he frowned. "Junior knows him?"

"No. Richard. I think they were in the same class," Nydia said as she put her hand over her forehead and scrunched her eyes closed. "Give me a minute. Let me think." After a moment she let her hand drop and she began to pull pieces off her napkin. After playing with it for a minute or two, Nydia stopped and looked up with her eyes open wide. "I remember."

"What?" Duncan and Jo said at the same time.

"Richard. Richard and Todd were close buddies from when they were in about the third grade. I didn't connect it because Richard always called him 'Butch,' not Todd."

"Just how close were they?" Jo's gut was telling her that Todd stayed off the radar so long because of their relationship.

"They were best friends from what I remember. The two of them were always hanging out together. Mom wasn't a fan of Butch, I mean Todd, so for the most part they weren't at our house. When they got older, they went camping out at Smith Point Beach all the time. Richard liked the surf fishing there. When they were old enough to drive, Richard and Butch would disappear for days on end. They would load up this old RV my dad stored in the backyard and go out."

"Your dad had an RV?" Duncan asked.

"Can you remember anything about it?" Jo asked.

"I...I'm not sure," Nydia said. "It's been so long. Why? What's going on? Did I say something wrong?"

The waitress came to the table to deliver their food. Jo took the moment to think about what Nydia told them. *What are the chances it's the same RV? It would have to be twenty years old or more by now. But, if we can connect it back to Nydia's brother, that would answer a lot of questions and toast him.*

"Hey, guys, let's take a break. We can pick this up after we finish dinner. All of us have had a long day. We can take a breather and regroup," Duncan said.

Jo looked at him, puzzled by his statement. He gave a slight nod toward Nydia who was looking at the plate in front of her with a frown. Jo glanced at Nydia and turned back with a slight tilt of her head. She saw how nervous Nydia had become. Duncan was right. Giving her a break would give Nydia time to calm down and gather her thoughts. The chances of her remembering more grew if she was in a better frame of mind.

They spent the next hour eating and relaxing, each telling funny stories about what was happening in their lives. The most amusing was the story Jo told about the date Ellie had with a male nurse at the hospital. The disaster it turned into was a comedy of errors, mostly because he came out as gay several weeks later. The check arrived soon after they had finished their slices of pie. Jo took her wallet out before anyone else had the opportunity.

"My treat. We've all had hard days, so think of this as a gift. You guys deserve it."

"Thank you, honey," Nydia said with a gentle touch to the small of Jo's back as they stood to leave.

"I knew I kept you as my partner for a reason," Duncan said and let out a small chuckle.

As she opened the door, Jo shot a good-hearted glare and wry grin in his direction. "Is that why? I should have known." Her smile disappeared. "But you may change your mind in a sec." Jo turned to Nydia. "I'd like to hear more of what you remember. Would you mind ruining the rest of your day? I think we should get an official statement about this. You agree, Duncan?"

"Shit. You're right. If I weren't so tired, I would have known that was coming. Let me just call Maddy to say goodnight," Duncan said as he let the door close behind them.

"Are you up for it, love?" Jo asked. She relaxed when Nydia smiled.

"I can do that, honey. Though I don't understand the need to be this formal about it, but if it helps you out, sure," Nydia said with a smile.

"Okay. Duncan, we'll meet you back at the station. We can all take our own cars." She turned to Nydia and took her hand.

"I'll see you later," Duncan said as he turned and walked away, pulling his cellphone out of his pocket.

Jo and Nydia made their way to Jo's car in silence. Jo didn't feel the need to say anything and watched as Duncan got into his car a few spots down from where she had parked and thought, I *feel bad. He had planned on trying to get up to see his wife tonight. My suggestion killed that idea.*

She shook her head. *Let me enjoy a moment before I have to go back to work.* Jo turned and put her hand on Nydia's hip, pulling her closer. She placed a gentle kiss on Nydiai's lips while she felt Nydia put a hand on the back of her neck and run her fingers into the hair at the nape of Jo's neck. The kiss lasted only a moment and Jo was sorry it ended. She stepped back but still rested her hands-on Nydia's waist.

"I love how you make me feel, Nydia. I want to tell you that with every fiber of my being, I love you. It might be cliché, but it's how I feel." Jo caressed Nydia's check with the backs of her fingers. Nydia's body shivered under her touch.

Nydia's eyes began to tear up. "I love you too. I never thought I would ever love someone, or they would love me. But then you came into my life."

"I'll always be here." Jo pulled Nydia into a strong hug and kissed the crown of her head. Let's go before Duncan starts wondering what happened to us. I'll meet you at the station."

"Okay." Nydia watched Jo get in her car and moved aside as Jo backed the car out. In her rearview mirror, she saw Nydia give her a small wave as Jo pulled away.

As Jo waited for traffic to clear, a slow smile came to her face. She was looking forward to afterwards. The smile faltered though when she thought about having to talk about Todd Donnelly. Jo suspected they were going to discover much more. Jo turned onto Main Road as Nydia pulled out behind her.

Chapter Twenty-six

JO KNEW THE TALK at dinner was only the beginning of something bigger. She could feel it in everything that made her a cop, enough to put Nydia through a formal interview. *I just hope we both survive this.* Jo looked through the one-way glass, as Duncan entered the interview room carrying two cups of coffee. She listened to their conversation through the speaker.

"Thanks for the coffee, Duncan," Nydia said. "After today, I need the caffeine."

Duncan gave her a small smile. "Yeah, me too." He took a sip from his cup and sat across from her.

Jo watched Nydia as Duncan pulled out a notepad. Nydia fidgeted in the chair. Jo wanted to hold Nydia's hand, but she couldn't this time. Jo had to put on her shield, even if it meant it covered her heart for a short period of time. Getting to the bottom of the Donnelly case was too important to let it slip away.

Nydia glanced around the dingy room. Jo knew the room by heart. The overhead lighting was recessed and covered by wire mesh. The cement brick walls were painted a dull beige color. The only furniture in the room was the table and four metal chairs. The ones across from Duncan were bolted to the floor to prevent anyone from using them as a weapon. The room was dismal, which was how it was meant to be. It put suspects and witnesses at a disadvantage, but gave the detectives the ability to lead the conversation.

Duncan sat at the end of the table while Nydia sat facing Jo. Nydia's brows scrunched together over the bridge of her nose as she looked at the one-way mirrored glass. He gave Nydia a small smile. Jo had seen him use it a thousand times to reassure witnesses and victims. It made him look less intimidating.

"Let's start with you taking a nice relaxing breath. You look like I'm the Inquisition." Duncan chuckled.

Nydia let out a long sigh. "Okay. I think I'm ready."

"Great. I'm going to ask some basic questions first. This way we can put them in your statement.

"Let's start. Your name is Nydia Rogers?"

"Yes."

"Okay, Nydia, what's your relationship to Richard Rogers?"

"He's my older brother."

"And he's a detective in Riverview? Are you in contact with your brother?"

"Yes, he is. But no, we haven't spoken in years."

"Can you tell us what you know about the association between Richard and Todd Donnelly?"

"He was friends with a Todd Donnelly while we were in school, but as I said before he usually called him 'Butch.'"

"Can you describe him or tell us anything about him that might help us identify him as the same person we have in custody now?"

"Uhm..." Nydia stared at the ceiling for a few moments before looking back at Duncan. "When he graduated high school, he celebrated by getting a tattoo on his left shoulder. It was a shark, the school mascot. He showed it off every chance he had."

Duncan wrote it down, but Jo already knew the suspect Todd had a similar tattoo. "You sure?"

"Yeah, because Richard wanted one as well, but Dad got livid and said no."

Duncan pulled several photos out of the folder in front of him. "Do any of these look like the tattoo you remember?"

Nydia pointed to the image closest to Duncan. "Yeah, that's it. It wasn't that well done, and had the school slogan written under it."

"Can you remember when Todd and your brother became friends?"

Nydia took a sip of her coffee and set the cup on the table. Jo watched her, and could see the slight nervous movements in her hands as she picked away at a spot on the table, and then moved her fingertips across it in a steady side to side motion.

Jo didn't see it as a good sign. She didn't think she had ever seen Nydia look apprehensive. She had been angry, assertive, strong-minded, unsure, and upset, but Jo had never seen her this nervous.

Duncan must have noticed it too. "We're not here to trap you or do anything that would go against you, Nydia. We just want to get some information about Richard and Todd. We're on your side."

Nydia took a deep breath and looked at the mirror. She gave a slight smile. It was enough for Jo to see Nydia was aware Jo was watching. Nydia squared her shoulders, took another deep breath, and looked directly at Duncan. "I don't know how much Jo has told you, but

I didn't get along with Richard as a kid. I tried to ignore most of what he did. That included his friends." Nydia's brow furrowed and her nose crinkled up. "I know they met in elementary school, third grade, I think. I always got the sense, when he was around, that my mother didn't approve of Todd. As Richard got older, she spent a good deal of time arguing with Richard when Todd was at the house."

Nydia stopped for a moment. She picked her cup up. "Whether that was because of Todd, Richard, or the both of them together, I don't know. After my mother died, the two of them seemed to spend a great deal of time in detention."

There was a sadness in her voice and Jo had to fight the urge to reach out to her. This was business and right now she was a cop, not Nydia's lover. She was here on behalf of Barbara.

"Richard grew angry and hard after Mom was gone. I never understood why. Now, it's too late to try. I stopped trying to understand it decades ago." Nydia stopped talking for a moment and looked lost in thought. "They stayed friends after high school. Richard went to the community college, and then started at the Police Academy. As I recall, Todd went to work for his father at his garage over in Flanders. I left for college about that time."

"Have you seen them since then?" Duncan asked as he finished a notation on his pad.

"I haven't had any contact with either of them since then. Except for the occasional run in with Richard through work. I see him around town on occasion. But that's rare." Nydia slid the coffee cup back and forth along the top of the table. She stopped and took a sip. Although her voice was clipped, the tension in her posture was less noticeable. Jo hoped she was starting to relax.

"When was the last time you think you saw your brother Richard?" Duncan asked.

"Oh, geez. I have no idea. Let me think a moment," Nydia said. She leaned back in her chair and looked up again. After a few seconds, she looked at Duncan, her eyes wide. "I know. I saw him about five months ago in the grocery store, the one on Main Road over in Mattituck. I remember because I was on my way to my friend Trudy's for a July fourth barbeque, and I needed to pick up the soda and beer. I saw him in one of the aisles on my way to check out."

"Did you talk to him at all?"

"God, no," Nydia said. "I haven't had a casual conversation with him since I left home. If I had to talk to him, it would have been about a patient."

There was something new in Nydia's voice, something Jo couldn't recognize. *I can't tell if it's anger or resignation. Either one is better than the hurt I always heard before now. Her family isn't worthy of her and she never deserved what they did to her.*

"Have you seen Richard and Todd Donnelly together since college?" Duncan asked.

"Uhm. I think so. About a year ago."

"Where?"

"It's kind of odd that I even saw them. It was one of the nurse's birthday and the rest of the staff was going to Duggar's to celebrate. I normally would have passed, but Trudy convinced me at the last minute to go. She thought I was being a bit anti-social in my life at that point. Rather than argue with her, I went along."

"How did they seem to you? Friendly? Businesslike?"

"I'd say very friendly, thinking about it now. After the surprise of seeing Richard, I tried to keep out of view. The last thing I wanted was some kind of run in with him. I spent most of the time ignoring them.

"I remember that they were laughing. Carrying on. You know, being loud and obnoxious. I assumed they'd had a few drinks when I saw them. I didn't pay them much attention and lost track of them. I can't recall seeing either again."

"So, they seemed close."

"They seemed drunk and rowdy. Carrying on, being loud as I said, and harassing the waitress. I could hear them from across the bar. I didn't want to pay attention, but it was impossible not to."

"Did you see them leave?"

"No. We stayed until about twelve thirty. When we left, I caught sight of them on the other side of the bar. They looked pretty toasted."

"You stated previously that Richard and Todd were friends from childhood. Did you spend a great deal of time with them, together, or alone?"

"No. Neither really cared about me once my mom was gone. Most of my time was focused on keeping my head below the radar of my dad and brothers."

Duncan looked up from his pad. "You said your dad had an RV?"

Nydia's brow furrowed. Her voice took on a guarded tone. "Yes. We went camping when I was young. I don't understand why you would be interested in it."

Duncan ignored her question and asked his own. "You mentioned earlier today that your brother Richard and Todd used it."

"Yeah. Once they could drive, they would go out camping."

"Where did they tend to go?"

"Smith Point. I think I explained that before." Nydia started tapping her finger on the surface of the table.

"I know. I just need you to repeat it again for our records. I'm sorry, Nydia. I know it can be confusing."

"It is. I don't understand why you need all this information. It was years ago."

"I can't explain, Nydia. I apologize. I can tell you it will help Barbara Donnelly as part of our on-going investigation, if that helps." Duncan set his pen down.

"This has to do with Todd?"

"Yes. It may help our case with him. Are you willing to continue for us?" he asked, picking up the pen.

"Yeah. Uhm. Okay."

Nydia straightened up in the chair. Her demeanor was changing and Jo hoped it wasn't a bad sign. She had seen witnesses do it before, usually, right before they shut down. She had a desperate need to go in and reassure her. *But that would invalidate the interview. I can't risk that, not when we are so close to finding out the truth*. She had to watch with a wall separating them.

"They went to The Point every few weeks to go fishing. As they got older, before I went to college, it became once every month or two. Richard was busy with the police academy. Todd, I think he got married shortly after high school. He started working for his father. After that, I don't know. I never went home after I left, so I have no idea."

"Going back to the RV. Can you remember anything about the RV itself? Does your father still have it?" Duncan leaned toward Nydia.

"I have no idea if he does or not." Nydia's tone was one Jo had come to recognize as defensive.

"As I said, I haven't spoken to my family since I left for college. I know it was a Winnebago. I remember because when he got the thing, Dad spent a week reading the manual. It was tan and white. Other than that, I really don't know anything."

Jo tracked Nydia's eyes as she watched Duncan enter her answers onto his pad.

"I don't understand why you're interested in Richard and an old RV of my dad's. Did Richard do something?" Nydia asked in a hard, demanding tone that Jo had heard her use at the hospital.

This was exactly what Jo feared. Nydia was growing tenser by the moment. Her hands were clenched into fists on the table. Her posture was stiff, and she was glaring at Duncan. Her anger was coming to the surface.

"Nydia, I can't really explain other than to say Richard's and Todd's friendship may have led Richard to make some poor choices." Duncan tried to reassure her.

"So, wait. You're going to use this against Richard. Look, I may not like my brother, or have any love lost for him, but that doesn't mean I want him in trouble. This sounds like you're setting him up for a criminal fall, Duncan. Is Jo in on this as well?"

"She's aware of the connection. We're both working the case. You know that," Duncan said in a gentle tone.

"So what? Was dinner just a way you could get information out of me?"

Jo could hear the incredulity in her voice.

"No. Of course not. We didn't even know you knew anything when we met up with you tonight."

"Well, I've given you everything I know. Do with it what you want to. Am I free to go?" Nydia pushed off the table and stood up.

Duncan tried to save the interview. "Nydia, be reasonable. You were always free to leave. It's not like we arrested you."

"No, but I get the sense I may not be as free to leave as I want, Duncan. Do you know what impact that sort of accusation will have on Richard and Steve Jr.'s career? Not to mention my Dad's. Plus, you're handing them more ammunition to hate me. Every chance they get they try to beat me down. Did Jo tell you that? Of course, she did. You're partners. I bet she told you as soon as she got the chance to, because that's how you people work. Nothing is sacred as long as it helps the case."

Jo watched helplessly as Duncan stood and tried to salvage her relationship from the disaster.

"That's not true and you know it, Nydia. Jo loves you. She never mentioned any of this. But I will tell you that if Richard got himself over a barrel, it's his fault and he deserves the blame. Not me and especially not Jo."

Jo's panic grew as she watched. *Duncan what the hell are you doing? I have to talk to her. I don't care what happens.*

Nydia stood motionless for a moment. "I'm done. Tell Jo I expected better of her." Before Duncan had a chance to say anything else, she walked past him.

Jo was already in the hallway headed toward them. She almost collided with Nydia as she stormed out of the interview room. Jo took hold of Nydia by the shoulder to stop her walking past her. "Nydia, wait. You don't understand. We—"

"Let go of me, Detective Powers," Nydia said between clenched teeth.

Jo let her go and she felt as if her heart wrenched as she did. "Nydia, you know I love you. Why do you think I would throw that away for a case?"

"Because I do know you, Jo. I know making the case means everything to you. That's because of your father. You feel the need to rescue everyone you can. Was that the deal with me? Was I just someone else on your list of good deeds? I don't need your pity, and I don't need to be your charity case. If you want to get back at my brother at any cost so you can solve your case, do it on your own."

Nydia pushed past her, bumping Jo's arm with her shoulder.

Jo was stunned. She stood rooted in place. Unsure of what to do for the first time in years. The tears began to fall as she watched Nydia disappear through the door of the station. *I don't understand. She said she loved me. I thought she trusted me. That she understood who I am,* Jo thought. She barely noticed Duncan stand beside her. Nothing mattered except that Nydia was gone.

Chapter Twenty-seven

JO WALKED INTO THE station Monday morning with her head down and carrying a cup of coffee. She hadn't slept much the last few nights. Although she barely paid attention to where she was walking, she managed not to bump into anyone as she made her way to her desk. The burden of Friday weighed her down. Her mind wouldn't stop replaying the confrontation. When she made it to her desk, she fell into her chair with a large sigh.

"God. You look like crap," Duncan said, passing a plate to her.

Her stomach grumbled and she was sure Duncan had heard it. The smell of the toasted bagel and cream cheese was too much to withstand. *I'm hungry, tired, and heartbroken. At least I can fix the first,* she thought. The warmth of the bagel was soothing. It worked on the ache in her stomach but not her heart. She tried to stifle the yawn that came but failed.

"Did you manage to get any rest?" Duncan asked.

"What the fuck do you think?" Jo knew holding Duncan responsible wasn't fair, but she didn't know who to be angry at other than herself or Nydia. She couldn't get a clear thought on who to blame. *Whose fault was it? Do I blame Duncan for conducting the interview, or myself for pushing Nydia to do it?* Jo sighed. What she really wanted to do was blame Nydia. After all they had been through. Nydia promised she trusted Jo, believed she was a loving person and a good and devoted police officer. But the second things got tense and emotional, Nydia turned on Jo and shielded her brother.

Jo sat back in her chair and contemplated that. *Richard. Why in the world would Nydia defend him after the way he's treated her all these years? There was no love lost between them. They hadn't even been in touch for years. There has to be something going on here. Something I don't know about. Is it possible Nydia knows more about Richard and Todd and isn't telling us? No. I refuse to believe that, not after what Todd did to Barbara. Nydia saw it herself. But why would she protect her family after everything they've done to her and how they've treated her?*

Jo was too confused to think about it anymore.

She leaned forward resting her arms on the desk. "Did we get the documentation back on the RV we found Donnelly in?"

"Yeah. The title and registration came back to a Steven Rogers, Jr., over on Sound Avenue. Which happens to match Junior's address." Duncan passed a folder to her. "The forensics team from County found prints. They ran them last night and found a match to both Todd Donnelly and Richard Rogers."

"Shit. Does anyone else know about this? If word gets back to them or the Chief, we're done. Our careers will be over, and with no one to charge, everyone walks away clean." Jo dropped the folder on the desk where it landed with a thud.

"No, not yet. It was done up at County, and since we had an idea something might be up, I made sure the reports came to me directly. Nothing's in the system yet. I printed out the email. What you have there is the only proof in the building."

"Good thinking, buddy. I'm surprised about Junior though. I know he is a prick, but I never would have guessed he would cross the line in this big a way."

"Me too." Duncan's voice was low. "The interesting thing though, is none of the prints came back to him. Except for the RV being in his name, there's no proof he was ever in it."

Jo looked around the room. "Let's get out of here. I could use some fresh air, and I don't want to find out who our enemies may be in here." She stood up and grabbed the folder as Duncan stood and grabbed his jacket off the back of his chair and they left the building

***

Duncan parked the car in the beach parking lot and Jo got out alone. She stopped at the bench to take off her shoes and socks and rolled up her pants. The weather was cold but she didn't mind. Jo did it often. She made her way down to the shoreline and stared out over the Long Island Sound. The beach gave way to the calm water. There was no wind today and the small waves lapped at the shoreline.

She didn't bother to see if Duncan was coming. Jo knew he would stay in the car a bit longer. When they came to the town beach, it was so she could clear her head and think. Get her mind settled. When she reached the water's edge, she stretched her arms up to the sky and arched her back.

"Argh!" She screamed in frustration and followed it with a holler. "Fuck. Shit. Crap." Her arms dropped back to her side and she fell to her knees. Her energy was draining away, and she had no idea how to stop it.

"You're lucky no one's here. The local kiddies would have had quite the vocabulary lesson," Duncan said, coming up to stand beside her. "Though you may have scared the plovers. I may have to report you for harassing the wildlife."

Jo chuckled at his attempt to lighten the mood. "To hell with them, and it's not plover season anyway. Besides, it's the wrong shoreline, so there. This morning it's all about me," she said and smiled. Not a big one, but it lifted her spirit, if only a tad.

"Speaking of you—"

"No, let's not, please. I'd rather focus on work right now. I'll think later about Nydia. But thanks for the concern. Maddy has taught you well."

"Hey, I can do sensitive all by myself, thank you very much," Duncan said with an exaggerated pout.

"Yeah. Right." She chuckled as she stood up and dusted off her pants. "Seriously, though. What do you make of all this with the Rogers brothers and Todd?"

"I think you're right about Junior. This doesn't seem his style. I can definitely see him roughing up a perp and some other stuff, but this? This is on a whole 'nother level. Aiding and abetting a suspect who is facing a felony assault charge, maybe even attempted manslaughter, goes beyond what I would imagine for him."

"Yeah. But it does sound like Richard. I can practically smell him all over this. The problem is how do we prove it?"

"I have no idea," Duncan said. "We left the uniforms canvassing the Point. We're still waiting on their reports. I'm not holding my breath, but maybe they slipped up somewhere."

"The RV is in the County shop. We can take a look at it for ourselves once they're done with it."

"Okay." Duncan turned and stared at her.

After a few moments, she couldn't take it anymore. "Is there something else? You look like someone kicked your puppy."

"Have you heard from Nydia?" he asked, his voice gentle.

"I thought we weren't talking about this. No and I don't expect to." Jo looked back over the water. A few ducks landed while they talked. Watching them was peaceful, almost. "Hell, at this point I'm not sure what I want."

"Really? Why not? You guys are so head over heels for each other."

"I don't know. I think I'm just tired of defending who I am to her."

"Huh?"

"Ever since I met Nydia, it's been an on-going battle of trying to convince her I'm not this evil version of the police that she imagines. Each time I think we've beat her insecurities she takes a step backwards. Last night felt as if it was the last straw." Jo ran her hands up over the top of her head, pushing her hair back before putting her hands in her pockets.

"Why do you say that? You guys have come so far. I've seen you together."

"I don't know. Maybe I'm tired. Tired of this constant up and down of emotions. Can you really blame me?"

Duncan sighed. "No. Yes. I know that I don't think a lot of people would. Except yourself, because you know better than most how love is such hard work. Unless both people are willing to give in to it, then no amount of love is going to fix it. You've seen that firsthand. I believe that you love her, maybe even more than your job. I feel as if you're truly happy for the first time since I've known you, and we went to the Academy together, so that's a long time. I blame it on Nydia. That woman is good for you. She may have her faults, but who wouldn't, coming from that family."

"Yeah, but I think this time only one of us is willing to work on it. Every time I think we've made headway she changes her mind. That's not going to work."

"You should talk to her."

"Why? So, she can say 'sorry' again. I don't need that. If she doesn't trust me one hundred percent, then how can we succeed? You can't build a relationship without trust."

"No one gets one hundred percent. Maddy and I don't." Duncan held up his hand to stop Jo from speaking. "I know what you're going to say, but we're human beings and we make bad calls sometimes. We make mistakes. Because of that, in a relationship there is never going to be one hundred percent of anything. It sounds like Nydia has spent the majority of her life under her father's thumb. I know those people, and I know she has scars. She's suffered abuse from all three of those men. Can you really blame her for her mistrust in the police?"

"I never told you about that."

"Yeah, but I know them, and a person would have to be stupid not to have guessed it. Her father is a small-minded, hateful bastard. He's a racist, misogynistic, homophobic bully. If he didn't hurt his wife and Nydia in some way, then that is his only redeeming quality, but I doubt it. Richard is a carbon copy of his old man. Junior is a follower, a sheep."

"Argh," Jo pushed her hair back again, "you're right. I was happy. She made me happier than I've ever been. But I don't know what to do. If it was just that, maybe we could work it out, except it's not. She betrayed me. Why take Richard's side? Why protect him over believing my word, believing in me?"

Duncan put his hand on her arm. "Jo. We see it almost every day. I'm surprised you don't get it. People who suffer abuse, for as long as she did, don't come out unscathed. She probably has her reasons and they make sense to her. We just don't understand them."

"Maybe."

"Just think on it. Remember all those victims who kept a hope alive that their partner, husband, wife, or other family member wasn't as bad and horrible as they truly were. That if they loved them enough, or if acted a different way, then maybe they could still be redeemed somehow. Maybe you need to start thinking that Nydia didn't survive as unscathed as you did." He let her arm go and walked away.

Jo turned and watched as he got back in the car. "When the hell did he get so wise?"

Chapter Twenty-eight

"WHO PISSED IN YOUR cereal today?" Trudy asked. "You've been grumpy and on the verge of hostile all morning. I know Mondays suck, but I thought you were going to fire the new nurse for miscounting the used syringes. You know it was a newbie mistake and she's only been here a few days. You need to cut her some slack."

"Let's get one thing straight. I don't *have* to do anything. This is my department and I'll run it the way I see fit. I don't need you, or anyone else, telling me how it should get done." Nydia let the patient tablet fall heavily on the countertop. "If you're not happy with that, you can always transfer, or I can do it for you."

Trudy stood with her mouth agape. "I'm sorry. What did you just say? Because I could swear you just threatened my job, and I know you didn't mean to do that."

Nydia rested her elbows on the counter and placed her hands over her face. She took a deep breath and let it out slowly, repeating the action two more times, trying to gain some control of her thoughts. She slid her hands off her face and rested them on the counter.

"I'm sorry, Trudy. I shouldn't take my anger out on you, or anyone here for that matter. Jo and I got into a fight Friday night. I destroyed us and I don't think I can fix it this time, and to be honest, I'm not sure I want to." Nydia began to cry.

Trudy came around the desk and put her arm across Nydia's shoulders. "Come on. Let's get you somewhere private. No one needs to see this, and you obviously have a lot to talk about," she said in a comforting voice.

Comfort is something I don't rate right now, or ever. My chance for that kind of affection is over, Nydia thought. Trudy led her into the doctors' lounge and closed the door behind them. Nydia was glad the ER was mostly empty and no one was in here. She heard Trudy lock it. Before she knew what was happening, Trudy had her wrapped in a bear hug. As soon as she felt the warm embrace, she buried her face in Trudy's shoulder and began to sob. Trudy thrust a pile of napkins into her hand. Nydia pulled away, sniffling and blowing her nose.

I don't deserve a friend like Trudy. She has been my rock for so long. God, how did my life become so undone in a matter of an hour or two? I destroyed a potential lifetime of love in a matter of a few angry, hurtful moments, all because I lost faith in Jo, again.

Trudy guided her to the small couch against one wall, and began rubbing her back in large soothing circles. Nydia wiped her eyes and blew her nose again. Trudy handed her more napkins.

"I think you're going to need these," Trudy said, her voice soft and soothing. "You're both so happy. At least you were when you left on Friday. Do you want to tell me what's going on? What happened?"

"I don't know. I met up with Jo and Duncan at The Snack Bar. We were enjoying dinner when they mentioned they had caught Barbara Donnelly's husband, Todd." Nydia took in a breath and let it out as a sigh. "Thanks, by the way. I feel better talking to you about it. Maybe it will make sense."

"I'm always here for you. You must know that after all these years."

"Yeah, I do. I guess sometimes I need to be hit with a stick for a reminder."

Trudy smiled and covered Nydia's hands with her own for a brief moment. "Well, you can always count on me to have a stick handy. So, go on. What happened next?"

"I remembered my brother, Richard, knew a Todd Donnelly. They were pretty much best friends growing up. I didn't make the connection until they brought him up. Anyway, Jo and Duncan started asking questions about him and Richard. Stupid on my part, but I really didn't think much of it at the time. Not even when they asked me to talk to them at the station."

"Oh geez. Barbara Donnelly's husband is Todd Donnelly. I remember him. Together, your brother and Todd were a vile pair. But why take you to the station? That sounds strange."

"Jo said they wanted to take a formal statement. I should have known something was up right then." Nydia thought it over for a moment. *Why didn't I? It was right in front of me. Especially when Jo wasn't there. How stupid of me.*

"So, they questioned you there?"

"No. Just Duncan."

"That's kind of weird."

"Yes." Nydia's ire began to rise. "By the time I figured out what was happening, I felt ambushed."

"I don't understand. What did they want from you that caused all this?"

"We started off okay. Just some basic questions, but then Duncan started asking more about Richard. For instance, how did he know Todd? Had I seen them recently? But then I got a weird feeling I can't really explain.

"I told him about the night we went out for Janet's birthday celebration down at Duggar's. I mentioned seeing them together."

"Yeah. I remember. You talked about leaving and I made you stay. I said not to let him ruin a good night out."

"Right. Well, then Duncan's questions turned to my dad."

"Your dad? He came up? Why on earth would Duncan and Jo want to know about your dad?"

"Not my father, so much as his old RV. Remember we went on trips when I was a kid?"

"Sure. Before your mom died. But that was years ago. I wouldn't think he even still owned the thing."

"I don't know. I remember it was still running when I went to college. Richard and Todd were still going fishing and camping out at Smith Point Beach at the time. I told Duncan that and he seemed to get excited about it." Nydia felt her blood pressure rising at the memory. "After a few more questions about Richard, it suddenly dawned on me. Jo and Duncan were trying to connect Richard to helping Todd hide out and they were trying to use the little bit I know to do it."

Nydia slammed her hand on the arm of the couch. "They probably thought I would be willing to turn on Richard because of our history, which I'm sure Jo shared with Duncan. God. You should have seen her when I left. She just stood there, trying to come up with some lame excuse just so she could get me back in."

"Are you sure that's what it was?"

Nydia heard the disbelief in Trudy's voice. By the tone, she knew Trudy thought she was overreacting. But Nydia knew she wasn't. "You don't understand. Don't they realize what that would do? Not just to Richard, but to my father and Stevie? It would destroy their careers. If Jo and Duncan had their way, people would assume they knew about it and helped him. I couldn't do that to them, especially not Stevie" Nydia stood up.

"Whoa. Hold on a second. I think we need to take a few steps back on this. How did we go from talking about Richard to a complete family conspiracy pinned on your family by Duncan, and more importantly,

Jo?"

"Well, of course that was what they were trying to do."

"Was it? I'm not so sure. You're making a hell of a lot of assumptions here. And why the hell are you defending Richard and the rest of them?"

"But—"

"No 'buts.' The whole thing seems to have gotten way out of proportion, and if you would sit down, we can talk this through. I'm pretty sure Jo and Duncan are not on some baseless crusade to frame your entire family because they feel vindictive."

Nydia realized her hands were clenched. She spread her fingers out wide hoping her tension would release. *Could she be right? Is it possible I've contrived this whole thing?* Nydia took a moment to reflect on what she had said. *No. It's not. I was there. Trudy wasn't.* She sat back down. "You don't understand."

Nydia stared straight ahead, refusing to look her friend in the eye for fear she would see judgment staring back at her. Instead, she tried to convince herself she was right. *I'm not the one who should feel ashamed, Jo should.*

"No. You're right. I'm not understanding because I can't see why you're defending Richard of all people. Remember, I was there when you were growing up in that house. I'm the only one outside of those walls who knows it went well beyond emotional abuse. It was never bad enough to get you to a doctor or an ER, but it still happened. I'm pretty sure the only one who didn't put a bruise on you was Steven Jr."

Nydia gasped. "How would you know? I never told you."

"Please, Nydia. I wasn't blind. I saw the bruising. It wasn't all the time, but when you tried to hide it from me, I guessed. You would tell people you fell, when I knew for a fact you hadn't. Your dad would grab you hard enough that you had finger marks on your wrists. I never said anything because I was a stupid kid. I thought it would only make it worse if I did." Trudy laid a hand on Nydia's shoulder. "I'm sorry, honey. I should have spoken up for you. Let you confide in me at least. Been stronger and a better friend. You had no one after your mom died. I should have done something."

Tears were running down Nydia's face, dropping on her clenched hands. Now they were tears of fear instead of anger. She was afraid. She had always been afraid someone would find out; and now she knew Trudy had known too. She had known for years.

The thought scared her. *Oh my God, I've never told Jo about that. If*

I told her, what would she think of me? That I'm even more of a pathetic, weak victim. Too afraid to get out, like almost all the other cases she sees. But she got out. She's strong and self-confident, everything I'm not. But I had no one. She had her family. I had just me to rely on. I got out. I ran the only way I knew how and I succeeded. Am I still running?

Nydia began sobbing, as if the floodgates holding back years of emotions had opened. She didn't know how much time had passed when someone knocked on the door and jiggled the door handle.

"Go away," Trudy said. "I'll be out when I'm ready—unless you have an emergency. Do you?"

After a moment someone on the other side said, "No."

"Okay, then give me five minutes."

Nydia sat up and wiped at her runny nose with the sleeve of her lab coat. She dried her eyes, and wiped her face off with more napkins Trudy offered.

"Are you okay?" Trudy asked.

"No, but I will be. At least I hope so."

"You'll be fine. It's out. That's a start. What do you want to do? Do you want me to see if I can get someone in to cover for you? I may be able to get someone."

"No. Give me a few minutes to get myself together again. I'll be okay. I'm sorry for pushing you away before. I feel out of control right now and it's freaking me out a bit."

"I can't imagine how you're keeping it together after that, but I'll take your word that you'll be okay."

"I think so." Nydia looked at Trudy. "Do you think Jo knew? Do you think that's why she made all those accusations against Richard?"

"No, I don't think she did. I think she loves you and will still love you when you decide to tell her. As far as what she did, I can only suspect she was acting on good information. She must have in order to you in that position. It makes sense, doesn't it? If she thinks she has a case against Richard, she couldn't do the interview. Duncan would have to do it because she is in a relationship with you. She wouldn't risk what you two have on a whim, or because of some vindictive vendetta against him."

"You think so?" Nydia said in a small voice.

"I know so. I've seen the way she looks at you. That woman would move heaven and earth for you. What would you say about Jo when it comes to her work?"

"That she is good at it. She's gentle when she needs to be. She lives and breathes the motto of protect and serve. The job is everything to her. But isn't that the problem. Did she do it because of the job?"

Trudy took Nydia's hand. "Based on that, I bet if she is somehow accusing Richard of helping Todd, then you can be sure there is probably something to it. She is one of the finest cops I know."

Nydia saw the napkins in Trudy's lap. "Can I have some more of those? I think I could use them."

"Yeah, I think you could, too. Here." Trudy handed over the pile.

Nydia wiped her face again. "I know you're right about Jo and Richard. Deep down I know Jo wouldn't do something like that only to get even with him. But now I've reacted the same way I always seem to respond. I ran, and now I don't know what to do about it. I've hurt Jo too many times to fix it now. I've gone too far this time. I know it. Why would she believe me now when I try and apologize again? If it was me, I wouldn't." Nydia felt her eyes begin to sting once more, but held back the tears this time.

"It won't be easy. Nydia, you have to be honest with her. Now is the time to tell her the truth, all of it. Jo will understand. You just have to give her the chance, you can't do that if she doesn't know everything, and it's not fair to her either."

"I don't know what to say to her. 'I'm sorry' isn't going to make it better this time. I've said it on too many occasions for it to mean anything at this point."

"No. Not likely. But I'm sure whatever you do, in the end it will be enough, as long as it comes from your heart." Trudy tapped a finger over Nydia's chest.

After a moment, Nydia said, "I hope so."

"Come on. We have to get out of here. People are probably wondering what's going on."

"Yeah. I'm sure they are."

As they stood to leave, Nydia looked at Trudy. "I can't thank you enough, Trudy. For everything you did for me then, and that you still do now. You are the closest thing to family I have. I want you to know that." Nydia hugged her.

"No, not anymore. Jo is the closest you have now. But I'm willing to be second place to her. Come on, let's go." Trudy unlocked the door, and turned back to Nydia before she turned the knob. "Ignore everyone out there. None of this has to go beyond these doors."

"Okay. Except Jo. I need to talk to her right after shift is over. I doubt she will take my calls, but I have to try. I need to do this in person and to do that I have to get her to agree to see me. Showing up on her doorstep may make the situation worse."

"That sounds like a good idea. I'm sure you can work this out, Nydia. I believe in you two." Trudy opened the door and they both walked out.

Nydia didn't notice any staring or whispering by the staff, not that she would have. Her mind was already on how to go about fixing her relationship with Jo. She needed work to be over so she could go find her.

Chapter Twenty-nine

JO WALKED INTO THE detective room Monday morning, holding her coffee. Once she settled at her desk, she took a large swallow of the strong black coffee. Duncan's chair was still empty. She was glad she beat him to work. She wasn't in the mood to talk to anyone first thing. She wanted to brood for a few minutes.

She spent most of the night before wishing she could turn her phone off. However, since work needed her to be available, she had to listen to it ring every time Nydia called or texted. She finally blocked the number so it would go straight to voicemail.

The three hours' sleep she managed to get did little to improve her mood. *Right now, my life would be so much easier if I could just forget. Damn you, Duncan. Now I have no idea what to do. Could I forgive her? If she apologized today, could I be sure she meant it this time? To be honest, I don't know.*

She decided to focus on what she could fix and that was the Donnelly case. But it was proving tough. She woke up her computer and opened her inbox. She stared at the monitor, but her mind was thinking about Nydia. Jo jumped when a wadded piece of paper hit her in the forehead and landed on her blotter.

"You with me?" Duncan asked as he sat. "You can at least pretend to pay attention to me."

"Do that again and you won't want me to notice you."

"Ha. Empty threats. You love me and you know it." Duncan smiled.

"You're lucky I do or you'd be dead by now. Do we have anything new on the Donnelly matter?"

"You didn't check when you got here?"

"I started to. I got sidetracked." Jo looked away, pretending to be looking at papers on her desk.

"Well, since you look like shit, I guess we can cut you some slack. Does your appearance have anything to do with Nydia?"

"Let's not go there. If I can find a few other things to think of right now, that would be perfect."

"Okay. But you have to at some point. You can't spend the rest of your life wondering what could have been, buddy."

"I know, but not now. I spent enough time last night dwelling on the whole mess."

"I take it you didn't come up with any decisions?"

"Not a one. So, what do we have with Todd?"

"Let me check the files. See if any new reports came in."

Jo waited while he checked his email and the files.

"We have a report from one of the county uniforms. A man was seen leaving the RV the day before we got there. The general description fits with our other suspect, you know who, but not enough to ID him."

"Damn. Sorry I missed that." Jo said. "Hoping for the ID was a bit of a long shot, though. What we need is for Todd to talk. But I doubt that will happen. He seemed pretty sure of himself Friday."

"I agree. I'm confident he thinks he's still going to worm his way out of this. He won't hedge his bets against that."

"You're right. So, what now? Any ideas?"

"We could try our other suspect. Let him know we have an idea about what's going on. He might come out of the woodwork long enough to get caught with a bit of cheese," Jo said. "I'm sure Todd has gotten word to him already. I doubt he will put up with his current situation without it."

"Let me grab Richard's home address."

"Yeah. It's too early for the bars to be open yet, so we can probably find him there if he's not on the clock." Jo stood up and grabbed her coat as Duncan did the same. "Let's get this done."

"Right behind you."

***

The house Jo and Duncan pulled up to looked abandoned. The grass was overgrown, weeds grew through the gravel driveway, and debris was everywhere. The bushes along the front had grown past the windows, blocking the sun. A small sapling grew out of the gutter. She guessed anyone who lived like this either had a desperate need for money, or didn't give a crap.

Jo and Duncan walked slowly up to the side of the house to the only accessible door. Jo rang the doorbell. She wasn't surprised when she heard nothing inside. "Broken."

Duncan reached past her and banged on the door several times. "That should wake him up."

Jo smiled as she imagined a hungover Richard hearing that much noise. After a few moments, the door was flung open with force, making her jump back a few steps. Jo was surprised it hadn't gone flying.

"Who the fuck is beating on my fucking door?" Richard squinted his eyes against the glare of the sunlight. His eyes were bloodshot, and based on the rumpled look, he had slept in his clothes. The tell-tale smell of whiskey came off him that, she could smell it from where she stood. She took a step closer and there was a stench to his breath, making it obvious that it had been several days since he'd used a toothbrush.

Richard Rogers looked like a guy whose life was falling apart. It had only been a few days since she last caught sight of him at the station, but it was obvious that whatever hold he had on himself was slipping away, and fast, and was probably connected to Todd.

"Hi, Dick," Jo said.

"You! What the fuck do you want, dyke? And the name is Richard."

"Well, Dick."

The vein on his forehead stood out and his face flushed.

"I, actually we, came down to tell you we picked up Todd Donnelly. Funny enough, he was in an RV down at Smith Point Beach. We took him into custody Friday afternoon. It was all very exciting. You should've been there. Duncan, don't you have a picture with you? You know, of the vehicle in question?"

Duncan looked at her for a second, an eyebrow cocked. "Oh. Right. The pictures. Yeah, they're here somewhere. Let me check." He patted down his pockets. "Hmm. I can't seem to find them. They could be in the car. You want me to go look?"

"Nah. I'm sure Dick can picture it in his head. Right, Dick?"

Sweat broke out on Richard's brow and his eyes darted around. His face paled a little. Jo had seen this many times when questioning perps, usually right before they ran. She would bet her paycheck on Richard being knee deep with Todd. She'd give him just enough rope to hang himself.

"Anyway, we only stopped by to keep you up to date. Since you've been interested and everything. We wanted to let you know we should have all the information we need soon. So, until then, we'll let you get back to whatever you were doing." Jo looked at Duncan. "Come on Duncan, let's go get some lunch. I've built up an appetite, and we can wait for all those reports to come piling in."

As she got to the car, Jo took one last look at the house. It was as sad and pathetic as the man who lived there. She almost felt sorry for Richard. *What happened in his life that created this man?* She thought as she got in and started the car, then turned to Duncan. "Let's go talk to Junior while we're at it. We might as well shake the cage from both ends." Jo put the car in gear and headed for one of the local marinas.

***

Jo turned when Duncan tapped her shoulder with his. "Over there," he said with a nod. Junior was on the dock where his boat was tied up, talking to one of the captains. He hadn't seen them yet. "So, what's the plan?"

"My guess is if we throw him under the bus a little, Junior will try and find out what Richard is up to. You want to take the lead. If I do, I may kill him for what he did to Nydia last time we met."

"What happened?"

"Let's just say Nydia saved his homophobic ass from being kicked across the parking lot." Jo's fists clenched as she remembered the night by the river. "Lucky for him, and me too I guess, Nydia stopped me before things got out of hand."

"I'm glad she did." Duncan lead the way down the dock. "Okay well, let's get this done with. I'm interested to see what plays out between the two brothers."

"So am I."

Jo let Duncan walk ahead to give the impression he was acting as lead on the questioning. She hoped it would put Junior at ease.

"Hey, Junior," Duncan called out.

Junior's smile disappeared, replaced with disdain when he realized who was calling for him. "What do you two want? Can't you see I'm patrolling?"

"I can see you're running your mouth," Duncan said. "But that's beside the point. We came to ask you some questions regarding one of our investigations, unless you'd rather talk about why you're at your boat on duty."

"What the fuck do you want from me? Go worry about your own jobs. I'm busy."

"Wow. The vocabulary level you and Richard have is astounding. But that's not why we're here."

"Okay, other than being a dick, what do you want?"

"No. Dick is your brother." Jo couldn't resist the temptation.

Duncan put his hand on Junior's chest as he lunged forward. "Get off me, Reilly. I'm going to put that dyke in her place." He shot daggers at Jo with his eyes.

On some level, Jo was sure he had been through the same abuse in his early life as Nydia had. The difference was that she was able to cope with it and get out when she could. She wasn't unscathed, but she was still a warm, loving, caring person. That was why she did her job so well. Jo could see that now. She doubted the same was true for Junior. He was damaged too, but had chosen a different path. One that made him as wrong as his dad. He could have been a better person had he let Nydia love him the way she tried to. Despite what she thought about him now, she had another victim she needed to fight for—Barbara Donnelly.

"It's okay, Duncan. Let him go." Jo no longer had the heart to cause him more pain. "I'm not here to hurt you, Junior. We just wanted to ask you about an old RV your dad had."

Junior looked her up and down. "Why?"

Duncan lowered his arm. "Did you know it's registered in your name?"

"No. Why would it be? It was Richard's. Dad gave it to him when he graduated from the academy I think."

"Does he still use it?" Duncan asked.

"I have no idea. Actually, I thought it was gone. I haven't seen him with it in ages."

"We found it out at Smith Point County Beach with a suspect in it."

Junior realized what they were saying, and his eyes opened wide for a moment. "Whoa. Wait a minute. What the fuck are you talking about?"

"Todd Donnelly. We've been looking for him for several months now for assault and attempted murder. The charges will depend on how the ADA feels," Duncan said.

"Todd. I wouldn't help Todd if his life depended on it. He's scum in my book. So, whatever accusations you want to throw around, toss them somewhere else. I don't give a rat's ass about him."

"Well, if the RV is in your name—"

"I have no idea why it is. So why don't you go investigate that?"

"So, you had no idea?"

"No. I told you already."

"Okay. Jo, you finished here?" Duncan asked.

"Yeah. I'm finished."

The two turned and started to walk away. After a few yards, Jo looked back at Junior. "I'm sorry, Junior. I know Nydia misses you."

Junior looked at her for a moment. He shook his head as if clearing away some thought or memory. "I don't need your sorry. Go fuck yourself, Powers."

Jo heard the catch in his voice though his anger hid it well. She motioned to Duncan. "Come on. I think we caused enough damage here. There's nothing more we can gain." She didn't wait for him as she walked to the car without a word. She wasn't aware she was crying until she sat down in the driver's seat. She felt the wetness on her cheeks. Who they were for though, Jo didn't know.

Chapter Thirty

JO AND DUNCAN SAT in their unmarked vehicle outside the county jail next to the courthouse. They had parked in one of the farther spots behind a pole, but near the other unmarked county and police cars. They had a view of the entrance area and enough distance that no one could make them out.

"Do you think he'll show? It would sure be a bit stupid on his part. He must know we're on to him by now," Duncan said before taking another slug of his coffee.

"You saw Richard this morning. That's a man on his last legs. He's desperate enough to make this kind of mistake. I'm counting on it." Jo put the zoom lens camera to her eye. She scanned the parking area and the front of the jail. She sat up a bit straighter, and leaned her wrists on the steering wheel and for a few seconds the clicking of the camera was the only noise in the car.

Duncan peered out the front window in the direction she aimed the camera. "I'll be damned. He is that dumb. I guess Todd didn't have the money for his own bond."

Jo watched as Todd got into a car that had pulled up to the front walk. She snapped several shots of Richard as he drove them away. Now she had photos to prove the connection between the two men. "Grab the folder from the back, would you?" Jo opened the door and got out.

"Sure. Which judge is on today? We need to keep this tight. We both know if news gets back to Chief Rogers, we're screwed," Duncan said as they walked toward the building.

"Judge Moreland is on today. I trust him. As an ex-ADA, he's not going to cover for a dirty cop. Sealing the warrant shouldn't be hard."

***

Several hours later, Jo and Duncan sat in their car down the block from Richard's house but with sufficient distance to watch the side door. The light of the day was starting to wane as Duncan watched the front of the house in case there was activity. The search warrant gave them access to Richard's phone and allowed them to surveil the house. Jo was on the phone with an officer in the wire room at county headquarters, who was relaying real-time phone transcripts.

Keeping the warrant under wraps wasn't as difficult as she thought it would be. There were several of their fellow officers in town who had a bad taste in their mouth for Richard Rogers. She found three who were willing to suffer the consequences with the Chief, so long as Richard was taken down. She trusted them to do their jobs and to keep her and Duncan safe.

Two uniforms were on the next block to act as backup should they need them, the extra detective was there as well. They were in position behind Richard's place on foot. When this went down, she wanted to make sure it was done right. Normally, they would have more manpower, but now there were only a few she trusted enough for this. Even the county police had enough ties to Riverview to make her wary.

"Anything so far?" Jo asked Duncan, who was looking through the camera at the house.

"I can barely see through the windows, they're so dirty. I can see movement but can't make out who's who." Duncan lowered the camera. "Any word from the station?"

"Only that he got a few text messages from Junior. He's asking what's going on and what's Richard gotten him into. He mentioned Barbara, so it sounds like Junior's made the connection with Todd and Richard."

"What was Richard's response?"

"He told him not to worry about it, he has it under control, and it doesn't concern him. Pretty much what you would expect. He's setting him up to take the fall. My guess is he hopes to work this so he comes off clean. The question is how."

"It would take a miracle at this point. We have the photos of him with Todd. We have his prints in the RV, and at this point, I think Steven Jr. would throw him under the bus as well. Richard will be getting pretty desperate soon if something doesn't happen for him," Duncan said.

"Let's hope he's desperate enough to do something stupid."

Jo heard the muscle car before she saw it. The silver Dodge Charger came barreling down the street and careened into Richard's driveway, kicking up gravel along the way. It raised a cloud of dust as it came to a screeching halt. Jo and Duncan both cursed when Junior emerged, and slammed the door behind him.

"Shit," Jo said.

"Damn, there's no telling how Richard will respond to this," Duncan said.

"This changes the whole game plan. Get on the phone and let backup know we may have a potential hostage situation, or worse."

Jo watched Junior bang on the door. Richard swung the screen door open. and his brother shouldered his way past him and into the house. Jo could guess at Junior's thinking, but she had a better idea of Richard's. With him and Todd in that house and as wired as they were, anything could happen, and Junior would be in the crosshairs.

"Come on. Let's get a closer look. I have a bad feeling about this, and I want to be as close as possible," Jo said.

"Does the warrant let us?" Duncan asked.

"Yeah, we're covered. Don't worry. I'm not risking this case for anything. We'll do it by the book."

"Okay," Duncan said, as each opened their car door and closed it quietly behind them.

Using the overgrowth on the front of the house to shield them, the two made their way slowly toward the side door. The solid door was open, leaving only the screen door closed. As they got closer, Jo could hear yelling inside the house. Going by the volume level, things were heating up fast. Before they were able to get closer, they heard the sound of a gunshot.

"Quick get those uniforms in here. We're going to need a bus rolling," Duncan said.

Before Jo had a chance to stop him, he opened the door and went in.

"Shots fired! Shots fired! Officer may be down, Officer may be down," Jo yelled into her phone. She didn't wait for a response, and she had to assume the person shot could be Junior.

Jo entered the house with her gun drawn, she saw Todd laying on the kitchen floor. There was blood seeping through the hole in his shirt. His eyes were open but empty of any life. Richard swung the service gun in his hand toward her when she came into the room. Out of the corner of her eye, she saw Duncan with his gun aimed at Richard.

"Whoa! Let's calm down, Richard," Duncan said.

For a moment, Jo could only focus on the end of the gun. The hand holding it trembled.

"Richard, don't do it," Junior said from behind her.

"You had to get him involved, didn't you, Powers? It wasn't enough you tried to get me, but you went after the weak, sniveling kid too. Did you really think he had anything to do with this? He hasn't got the imagination of a gnat, or the guts. He's been a bawling pain in my ass since the day he was born. God, he's almost as useless as my sister is. At least he had his uses on occasion, unlike the perverted slag you've got."

"What are you talking about? I've covered for you from the beginning. Since mom died, I did everything you and dad wanted," Junior said.

"No, Junior. You followed orders like the stupid, needy puppy you are. You're as pathetic as the rest of the women in this family. Even mom was a waste of oxygen. It was a lucky day when Dad solved her. My life got so much better."

"What are you talking about?" Junior asked. "What did he do?"

"Please, are you really that stupid? Mom died during a fight with Dad. Did you really never wonder why there were all those cops at the house, but no investigation, no autopsy?"

"It was an accident. You said so," Junior said, his voice cracking.

"God but you're stupid. You've spent your whole life believing the shit we fed you. Fuck, you even turned on your own sister because we told you to."

Jo was stunned for a moment. *What the hell is he talking about? Is he saying Nydia's mother's death wasn't an accident? We'll have to figure it out later. Right now, my focus is on making sure no one else dies here.*

Jo noticed Richard's gun hand was lowered a bit. "Richard, it's done. There's no way this ends without you going out that door with cuffs on."

"There is if I kill you. You think your partner won't rush to your side if I shoot and Junior wouldn't dare try to stop me? He's too scared."

Jo took a deep breath to calm her nerves. "Let's not test that theory, Richard. I think you might be mistaken. Duncan may be my partner, but I don't know that I would stake your life on how much of a partner he is." Jo nodded her head toward Duncan.

"No. I think I've got him pegged just fine. I'm willing to risk that bet." Before Jo or Duncan could move, the gun came up and he fired.

Jo felt the burning sensation as the bullet hit her. The warm sticky feeling of blood dripping made her want to vomit, and for a moment, she felt dizzy. From where she landed on the floor, she could see Steven

Jr. and Duncan forcing Richard to the ground and the gun flying across the floor. She heard the click of the handcuffs and sirens in the distance. Soon the room was filled with EMTs and other police officers. She closed her eyes, hoping the pounding in her shoulder would stop.

Chapter Thirty-one

NYDIA CAME OUT OF the exam room and went to the nurses' station. "The patient in three needs to follow up with his regular doctor. I put in some stitches. He had his tetanus shot within the last two years, so he's good to go." She set the tablet on the counter. "Can you get the discharge packet together, Trudy? I'll sign it when you've got it. Thanks."

Before Trudy could answer, the sound of the emergency radio interrupted them. "Riverview Ambulance to Riverview Hospital, coming in with Riverview PD. Gunshot wound to the upper shoulder. ETA five minutes."

That was the last Nydia heard. She rushed into the trauma room as she heard the call for the trauma team go out. Within moments, everyone required was getting ready. They only needed the patient.

Trudy came into the room. "The ambulance is one minute out."

"Okay. Let's go meet it." Nydia couldn't get the thought out of her head, *Please, don't let it be Jo, please.* Before Nydia had time to think, she heard the backup alarm for the ambulance. She stood alongside the ER doors, and watched when the ambulance doors opened and the EMTs brought out a gurney. She saw the blue police uniformed legs and breathed a sigh of relief. But it was short-lived.

"Stevie?"

Steve Jr. turned his head toward her, but when he saw Nydia he twisted away with a grimace. Nydia stood in stunned silence for a moment.

"Do you need me to get one of the other doctors? The EMT said the bullet grazed his shoulder. It's something one of the other doctors can take care of," Trudy asked.

Nydia shook her head and followed the gurney down the hall. "No. It's okay. I'll look after him. If he lets me." *I'll always look after him*, she thought. Nydia watched as one of the nurses finished cutting the bloodstained shirt off. The wound was covered with a bandage from the EMTs.

Nydia heard the vitals as her team called them out. Except for his heart rate and blood pressure, things seemed okay. She knew the higher than normal numbers were probably caused by the stress of the situation. She stood next to the bed and he looked up at her. His face reminded her of when he was her scared little brother. She placed her hand over his. "It will be okay, Stevie. You'll be fine."

Tears rolled down the side of his face. "No one's called me that in years. You and mom were the only ones. Don't be nice to me now, Nydia. I don't deserve it."

Nydia ran the back of her fingers across his cheek. "Yeah. How about we get a look at that arm? We can talk about the rest later," she said in a soft voice.

He grimaced when she touched his wounded shoulder. Trudy handed her the scissors when she put out a hand for them.

"Thanks."

"Anything you need," Trudy said.

"I appreciate it." Nydia glanced back at her. "Thanks, for being a friend too." She cut the bandage off to examine the wound. It was deep and a steady stream of blood oozed from it. She looked at Stevie again. "You're lucky. It looks like the bullet missed your deep tissue. You'll need some stitches though. I can fix this up easy. Would you feel better if I asked the others to leave?"

Stevie nodded. "If you can, please," he murmured.

"Sure."

"Thanks, Nydia."

Nydia turned to the rest of the staff. "Can we clear everyone out?" She waited until they all left to turn her attention back to Stevie.

"I'm sorry," he said.

"Nothing to be sorry about. You got hurt and—"

"No, not that. I'm sorry for everything, all of it. The last twenty years is what I'm sorry for. I've treated you like shit and I don't deserve your kindness. I did what Dad and Richard told me to. I was too weak to fight them, and it cost you." Stevie's tears ran down his face. He raised his good arm and wiped them away.

"You weren't weak, Stevie, you were a young boy. It was my fault. I should have protected you better."

"No, it wasn't. There was nothing you could have done. You needed to protect yourself. Two against one was never a fair fight. We both lost in the end. I believed they loved me, Nydia, and I was an idiot."

Nydia put the suture kit down and brushed the hair off his forehead. "No, you weren't. I understand what you're saying, Stevie. Once Mom was gone, there was no one for us. There was never going to be a savior at the end of our story. It was only you and me, and we were never a match against them."

"Today Richard showed that everything he ever said to me was a lie. He never loved me, and I doubt Dad does either. In fact, he's probably going to blame me for Richard."

"What happened to Richard?" Nydia asked in a soothing voice as she picked up the syringe. "This is going to burn but try and keep still."

Stevie let out a hiss as she injected the Lidocaine. She put the needle down and placed gauze under the area to catch the dripping blood.

"We have to wait a few minutes for this to kick in."

There was silence for several moments. Nydia saw Stevie's brows furrow. As a child, she knew it meant he was thinking about how to say something. It reminded her of him when he was six and tried to tell her he had broken her favorite toy; one her mother gave her. "So, do you want to tell me what happened?"

"Richard shot me."

"What? Why in the hell would he do that?"

"I went to his place to confront him about the RV Dad used to have. Somehow, it was registered under my name. Detectives Powers and Reilly came to question me about it. I stewed on it and went to talk to him this afternoon."

"I don't understand. What were Jo and Duncan scheming up? They've been after Richard ever since they found out he knew Todd. I should have expected something like this from her. I mean, them. They were probably hoping to get information from you too."

"Nydia, you have it all wrong. She was right about Richard all along. He was helping Todd by hiding him in the RV out at Smith Point. It was all a setup. If Todd got caught, it would fall back to me because of the registration. He used me."

"But why would he do that? Why did he shoot you?"

"Because he is still the monster he always was. He doesn't deserve your protection, Nydia. He never did." Stevie sighed. "I covered up most of the crap he did over the years, but this was going too far. You want to beat on a couple of perps—that's one thing, but to harbor a fugitive who almost killed his wife, is another. I wasn't going to stand for that. Not after Mom."

"Thank you, Stevie," Nydia said in a soft voice.

"Please don't say that. I've done a lot of awful stuff in this uniform. I've disgraced it. But not Powers and Reilly. They do the job and do it right."

Oh my God. I stood up for Richard. What must Jo think of me now? Nydia thought. She began to suture the wound. "What happened?" Nydia asked.

"When I barged in, Richard and Todd were arguing. Richard said he knew a doctor here who could make it look natural."

"Make what look natural?"

"Barbara's death."

"What?" Trudy said.

Nydia was so engrossed in what she was doing and Steven's explanation, that she hadn't heard Trudy come in.

"What Doctor?" Trudy asked.

"I just caught the beginning of it. God-something."

"Goddard?" Nydia asked, looking at Trudy as she set a tablet next to her.

"Maybe. He cut off when I came in. But that's what I overheard as I went in."

"I still don't understand what happened." Nydia tied the last knot. Trudy handed her the scissors to cut the suture thread.

Stevie got quiet and watched as Nydia finished up. After she placed a new bandage on the wound, she stood up so she could have a better look at his face. "Go on and finish, Stevie. What happened?" she said in a calm, gentle tone. Nydia heard Trudy leave the room when the door closed softly behind her.

His voice trembled. "It was bad, Nydia. I've never been that scared. Not even of Dad." He sounded so small and afraid. But she let him go on. "It got out of control so fast. I barged in and Richard immediately drew his service weapon. Todd told him to stop, that the plan was stupid, and would never work. He told Richard he was going to turn himself in. Richard said over his dead body. Then he shot him. Right in front of me. He shot him, as if it was nothing. I knew he was dead before he hit the floor, there was so much blood everywhere. Then Richard aimed it at me. I knew in that moment he would do it, and without thinking twice he'd kill me." Stevie let out a sob and took a moment to get himself together.

"Before he had a chance, though, Reilly barged through the door. I was backed up against the wall. Richard pointed the gun at him, but

Reilly moved away and had his gun already pointed at Richard. I told Richard to stop. But then Powers came in. She tried to play Richard, but he didn't fall for it. He took a shot at her. He hit us both. Reilly tackled Richard, and I did what I could to help him cuff him. He's probably at the station by now."

"Jo was shot? But where? Where is she?"

"I don't know. I assumed she was here or would be, by now."

Nydia barely heard his response as she jerked the door open. She ran up to Trudy. "Steve said Jo was shot. Where is she? Did she come in?"

"No. If she was here, I would have come and got you," Trudy said.

Nydia took her phone out of her pocket and tapped Jo's contact. Jo didn't answer, and her call went to voicemail. She tried again with the same result.

"Try Duncan," Trudy said.

"Of course." Nydia dialed his number. On the second try he answered.

"Reilly."

"Hi, Duncan. It's Nydia. Where's Jo? Steve said she was shot."

"Calm down, Nydia, please? She was hurt, but the EMTs saw to her. Despite procedure, Jo refused any medical care past a bandage. When they insisted, she asked to be transported to Greenport. She called a few minutes ago to say she finished and left. She has time before she needs to make a statement to Internal Affairs, so I assume she's on her way home. I'm sure if it's more serious than Jo is letting on, Ellie will make her come in."

"Oh my God. I have to talk to her, Duncan. I need to see her."

"I don't know that's such a good idea right now, Nydia. She was pretty shaken."

"I have to." Nydia disconnected the call before he had a chance to reply. She turned to Trudy. "I—"

"I know. Go find her. Your shift ended five minutes ago anyway, and I'm sure Dr. Stephenson will understand. If Dr. Jarvis has any questions one of the other staff or I can't answer, I'll have her give you a call. Now go."

"Thanks." Nydia kissed Trudy on the cheek.

Trudy didn't have a chance to reply. Nydia was gone and in and out of her office, and on her way out the door in a matter of moments.

***

Jo sat on the bench, watching the small waves of the Long Island Sound crash at the shoreline. The sun was beginning to set and the chill in the air was growing. She looked to the west and saw it would be getting dark soon. The last rays of the sun were starting. *I don't care. It's not like I have anywhere to be, or someone special to see. No, not after today. Once Junior tells her about Richard, I'm sure Nydia will never want to see me again, let alone talk to me, or love me.*

She pulled her coat closed and felt a twinge in her arm that made her hiss. "Damn, that hurts."

"I bet it does," a voice behind her said.

Jo looked up, squinting against the setting sun. "Nydia?"

"Yeah. Do you mind if I sit with you?"

"No." Jo turned her gaze as Nydia stepped around in front of her. "What are you doing here?"

Nydia took a seat at the opposite end of the bench. "I went to your house. Ellie said you never came home. When I told her you were upset with me, she said you like to come down here to sit and think. To calm down and watch the sunsets."

"Oh." Jo went back to watching the waves.

"Jo, Stevie, I mean Junior, told me what happened."

"I'm sure he did. Then you can also blame me for Richard. He's being arrested for murdering Todd Donnelly, and conspiracy to commit murder on Barbara Donnelly's case. Plus, the aiding and abetting charges."

"Steve said you stood in front of him. That you protected him from Richard."

"Is that what he said?" Jo kept her tone flat. She could feel the lump in her throat building and didn't want it to come out. If it did, she would breakdown in front of Nydia, and she refused to let that happen.

"Yes. Then he said you got hurt. That's why I came looking for you."

"Well, as you can see, I'm fine. You can go now. You've done your duty."

"No, I won't. Because, I also came to apologize and say, I'm sorry. I never should have doubted you."

"But you did, Nydia. Again." Jo felt her voice crack and swallowed.

"I know. I am so sorry, and I know I don't deserve for you to believe me."

"Why should I, Nydia? Every time circumstances got questionable, you assumed I was the bad guy. That I was just like your family. I'm not, and honestly, I'm tired. I don't know how else to prove it to you."

"You don't have to. I've treated you badly. I never should have doubted you."

"Look, Nydia. I understand that you grew up abused. I get that. But I don't know if you're ever going to trust me enough to make us work as a relationship, as partners."

"I'm sorry, Jo. I didn't realize what I was doing. Trudy made me see it. You're right, I did lump you in with them, and I never should have. It's just that I was scared."

"Of me?"

"Yes. No. Jo, I'm sorry. I don't know how else to say it. I just don't know how to put the amount of regret I have about what I've done to you into words." Tears started to fall down her cheeks.

Jo reached out and brushed some away. "Don't cry, honey."

As soon as she said the words, Nydia began sobbing. Jo gathered her in her arms and tucked Nydia's head under her chin. Ignoring her own pain, she began making smooth, gentle circles on her back with her good hand, while uttering gentle words.

"It's okay, Nydia. You'll be okay."

"No. I won't. Not without you. I've messed us up, and I hurt you."

"I forgive you, Nydia. I do. It's that I don't know if I can risk my heart anymore."

After a few moments, Nydia sniffled and looked up at Jo. Her eyes were still wet and red as she wiped her nose with her sleeve. "I shouldn't ask you to, but I will. I need you to see why I did it. Maybe then you can give us another chance."

"Okay."

"Ever since my mother died, I've felt abandoned. She left me. She died and left me with my father and his emotional and physical abuse."

Jo looked up at her, her eyes wide. Nydia could see she wanted to say something. "Before you say anything let me get this out."

"The man who was supposed to love and protect me. Then Richard, my big brother, the person who should have looked out for me, turned on me instead. He was as bad as my father was. Whether he was born mean, or my father made him that way, I don't know. I probably never will, but it doesn't matter, because the result was the same.

"Then there was Stevie. My baby brother. I promised myself I would never let them hurt him. I tried. I tried so hard to protect him. But it wasn't enough. Soon he left me too. They took him to that place where I couldn't reach him anymore. He took their side, and that was that. Everyone I ever loved, or who was supposed to love me, left.

Jo reached for her again. “Oh, babe—.”

“No, let me finish. Please?” Nydia sat up straighter and squared her shoulders.

“Okay.”

“Then you came into my life. I felt things for you I’ve never felt for anyone. I fought it, but eventually realized I was falling in love with you. That was the scariest thought I ever had. You suddenly had power over my heart that no one else ever had before. With a mere touch or word, you could destroy me. You, Jo Powers, could destroy my heart beyond repair.”

“I never would.”

“I know that. I see that now. But I didn’t then. All I knew was that I was afraid. I acted out of fear, striking out at you. I shouldn’t have. I’m sorry for everything I’ve done to you, Jo. I can’t take any of it back. I can promise that from this moment forward, I will do everything in my power to make sure that every moment. of every day. you know I love you, have faith in you, and most of all, trust you with my heart.”

“I love you, Nydia, with all my heart. I always have. I promise to love you, but I can only do that if you promise, as well.”

“I do. I will spend the rest of my life making sure I keep that promise.”

In the last light of the day, Jo leaned over and kissed the woman she loved, and always would.

Epilogue

NYDIA OPENED THE FRONT door to her house and called, "Hey Jo, I'm home. Are you here?" She set her keys in the bowl on the table next to the entryway.

"Yeah. I'm in the kitchen."

Nydia found Jo stirring something in a stockpot on the stove. "What's that? It smells fruity in here." She stood behind Jo, wrapping her arms around her waist. She laid her cheek on Jo's back and soaked up the warmth she was giving off.

"Mulled wine for tonight. Which will be done soon, so you're just in time. Everyone should be here any minute. I left Duncan finishing up some paperwork, but he called and said he left right after me. He was picking up Maddy and the kids."

Nydia stepped back from Jo. "Oh, I can't wait to see the baby. It's hard to believe she's almost a year old."

Jo turned around. "Yeah. It's been a good year for everyone, I think. It will be nice to have Christmas Eve here. It feels like home now that we're both living here. I love this house, and I love you." Jo placed a kiss on Nydia's cheek. "What kept you late at work?"

"Dr. Stephenson wanted to fill me in on Dr. Goddard, or should I say ex-doctor?"

"Definitely ex." Jo laughed as she turned back to the simmering concoction. "I don't think they let you practice after you get caught trying to poison a patient. If Stevie hadn't been willing to wear a wire, we never would have had enough to bring charges on Goddard. That reminds me, have you heard from Richard or your dad? I was hoping they might contact you this Christmas."

"No. Richard hasn't sent any word since the trial ended and Dad isn't talking to anyone. I guess he still blames Stevie and me that an investigation into Mom's death has been opened, and that it forced his resignation." Nydia took off her coat and hung it on the back of the chair. "But I don't want to think about any of them today. It's taken over a year to get to this point and I just want to enjoy Christmas with you, our family, and our friends. Speaking of family, Stevie should be by in time for dessert. He's working a late shift, but he's excited to spend the holiday with us."

"How does he like working patient transport?" Jo asked over her shoulder.

"He's enjoying it. He really has a good way with the patients, and it's giving him time to work on his L.P.N. certification. Is Ellie bringing her new boyfriend?"

Jo looked over her shoulder again. "First off, I'm pretty sure that coat doesn't belong there, and second, I don't know. Ellie's being very secretive about this one. I think it may be serious. I don't even know his name and they've been dating for four months already. I think that's the longest relationship she's had."

"Then it must be the real thing. I hope so. She deserves it."

"Yeah, me too." Jo turned back around. "Oh, I forgot to ask, since I got in so late last night. How was therapy yesterday?"

"Harsh. I think I cried the whole time. But as usual, it helped."

"I'm glad you're getting so much out of it."

"Me too. It makes me feel better and it helps me in the long run, because I love you and I want us to succeed." Nydia stood next to Jo, put her arm around her waist and kissed her on the cheek.

"We will. No. Let me correct that we are and—"

"Anyone home?" Ellie called from the front door.

"Yes, and your timing sucks, as usual," Jo said.

Nydia stole a kiss on Jo's lips before Ellie walked into the room.

"So, did you bring your mystery date?" Jo asked.

Ellie blushed.

"I'm going to assume by the redness of your face that you did. So, where is he?"

"Come on in, Cheri," Ellie said as she shifted her feet.

"Cheri?" Jo and Nydia asked in unison.

"Yes, Cheri."

A petite brunette woman walked through the doorway. She was about Ellie's age and had sparkling green eyes.

"Wow." Jo let out a low whistle as she turned the heat under the saucepan down.

"Hey. That's my date. Stop drooling." Ellie pouted.

Nydia nudged Jo in the ribs.

"I'm not drooling. Surprised is all," Jo said.

"Well. I'm not," Nydia said.

"You're not?" Ellie asked.

"No. I've seen the way you looked at some of the female staff.

Don't forget we work in the same place."

"She better not be looking anymore." Cheri grinned.

"Never again," Ellie said, smiling back.

"Hi, Cheri," Jo said, holding out her hand. She looked at Ellie as Cheri took her hand. "Does Mom know?"

"Not yet. I figured Christmas would be a good time to tell her."

"Please. You're her favorite child," Jo said.

"That's true," Ellie said.

Jo threw a dish towel at her.

"I hope you two are as happy as we are," Nydia said.

"Me too," both sisters said.

Nydia laughed. "Okay, now help before everyone else gets here." She watched as Ellie and Cheri picked up a pile of plates, and walked through the dining room doorway. Once out of sight, she sidled up to Jo. "I love you with all that I am."

"I love you too, honey." Jo leaned down, put her arms around Nydia, and kissed her.

Nydia kissed her back and prayed it expressed all her hopes and dreams for them. "I'm so happy you've included Stevie when you mentioned family earlier," Nydia said as she broke the kiss. She reached up and stroked Jo's cheek.

"He's done a lot to redeem himself. The way he convinced the women's shelter to let him volunteer as security for his community service was impressive. He's become family. Hell, even Mom has taken him under her wing," Jo said with a small laugh.

"I was hoping you were enjoying our new family dynamic." Nydia ran her fingers around the back of Jo's neck and began playing with the hair at the nape.

"I do."

Nydia leaned in and whispered into Jo's ear. "Would you be willing to expand it a bit more?" She felt the goose bumps rise on Jo's skin.

"Uhm...you make it hard to think when you do that."

"So, you want me to stop?"

"God. No." Jo said with a shudder in her voice.

Nydia knew she was playing dirty, but she was on a mission.

"What did you have in bed, uhm, I mean, mind?"

"Well, I thought we could start off with a...."

Jo took a step back and looked into Nydia's eyes. "Go ahead. Say it. Don't be scared."

"A kitten."

Jo took another step and knocked into the stove. She caught the handle of the pot as it began to shift. "What?"

"Hi, Jo. Hi, Nydia," Cassandra said walking in with a cardboard box. "I found this on the front porch. It was making quite the noise."

Nydia walked over and gave her a one-armed hug as she took the box. "Yes. I was just talking to Jo about it."

"You were?" Jo asked.

"Yup." Nydia took the cover off and handed the box to Jo.

Jo's brow furrowed as she looked into the box. She reached in and pulled out a tiny tuxedo kitten. She lifted it so they were eye to eye. The kitten mewed and reached its paw out to touch Jo's nose.

"I found her in the bushes behind the ER door. She's so tiny and cute. I couldn't leave her there."

Jo lifted the kitten up higher. "Her? Huh?" she said, as she brought the kitten down and let her snuggle into her chest.

"I thought we could keep her. I'm sure she wouldn't be too much trouble. A cat fits our hectic schedules, and—"

"Of course, we can. Whatever makes you happy. Plus, she is adorable as hell."

"Thank you so much." Nydia threw her arms around Jo.

Jo sidestepped her. "Hey, don't crush Dex."

"Dex?"

"Sure. She looks like a Dex, don't you think?"

"I love you so much, Jo Powers."

"For the rest of our lives, I hope."

"With every fiber of my being, and for all times." Nydia leaned in, careful not to crush Dex, and kissed Jo.

"Excuse me, is this how I taught you to cook Jocasta Powers? What you have on the stove is burning."

"Shit." Jo spun around, pulled the pot off the burner, and placed it on the other side of the stove. "Hi, Mom."

"Hi, to you too, sweetie. Merry Christmas, Nydia."

Nydia smiled. "It's a very merry and wonderful Christmas, Cassandra. I have everything I could wish for."

"As do I," Jo said. "Now, go entertain our guests. Dex and I have a meal to finish cooking. So, shoo. Both of you."

The End

About Ellen Hoil

Ellen Hoil lives in wine country on the North Fork of Long Island between The Sound and The Peconic Bay. "I can't imagine living anywhere that isn't near water and open space." When she isn't writing fiction, she does write for her other career as an in-house counsel attorney.

During her down time Ellen enjoys her hobbies of photography and getting involved in local politics. She is an ardent Sci-Fi geek and can be found at various conventions. "My philosophy on life is that failure is never the end, but only a temporary stopping off point for a new adventure."

Connect with Ellen

Email: e.hoil22@yahoo.com

Facebook: E Hoil Author

Note to Readers:

Thank you for reading a book from Desert Palm Press. We have made every effort to edit this book. However, typos do slip in. If you find an error in the text, please email lee@desertpalmpress.com so the issue can be corrected.

We appreciate you as a reader and want to ensure you enjoy the reading process. We would like you to consider posting a review on your preferred media sites and/or your blog or website.

For more information on upcoming releases, author interviews, contest, giveaways and more, please sign up for our newsletter and visit us as at Desert Palm Press: www.desertpalmpress.com and "Like" us on Facebook: Desert Palm Press.

Bright Blessings

Made in the USA
Middletown, DE
15 September 2022